Damon gestured for Carrie to step into the elevator. He stared straight ahead as the doors closed, determinedly not looking at her and resenting every moment of shared space and oxygen, especially when her scent infiltrated the air.

Her betrayal still burned within his gut and even if she was in possession of information that could be valuable, she had some nerve showing up to his territory and demanding an audience. Clearly she had inherited her father's gall!

Sour though he felt, Damon knew he could not roll the dice on whether she was being truthful, not with so much at stake.

Forty seconds later they arrived at his top-floor office and Damon secured the door behind them before striding briskly to stand behind his desk.

"You have five minutes. So whatever information you came here to impart, I suggest you speak quickly," he instructed with taciturn impatience.

Carrie stared back at him, her chin raised and her eyes clear. "I'm pregn

Rosie Maxwell has dreamed of being a writer since she was a little girl. Never happier than when she is lost in her own imagination, she is delighted that she finally has a legitimate reason to spend hours every day dreaming about handsome heroes and glamorous locations. In her spare time, she loves reading—everything from fiction to history to fashion—and doing yoga. She currently lives in the northwest of England.

This is Rosie Maxwell's debut book for Harlequin Presents—we hope that you enjoy it!

Rosie Maxwell

AN HEIR FOR THE VENGEFUL BILLIONAIRE

HARLEQUIN®
PRESENTS™

Recycling programs
for this product may
not exist in your area.

ISBN-13: 978-1-335-59197-5

An Heir for the Vengeful Billionaire

Copyright © 2023 by Rosie Maxwell

For questions and comments about the quality of this book,
please contact us at CustomerService@Harlequin.com.

Harlequin Enterprises ULC
22 Adelaide St. West, 41st Floor
Toronto, Ontario M5H 4E3, Canada
www.Harlequin.com

Printed in U.S.A.

AN HEIR FOR THE
VENGEFUL BILLIONAIRE

For my mum, whose love, belief and support
helped turn this dream into a reality.

CHAPTER ONE

*A car will pick you up at your hotel at
seven-thirty p.m. and bring you to the
unveiling of Chateau Margaux. I'll be
waiting there for you. Damon x*

CARRIE MILLER STARED at the words written in
elegant male script and then lifted her gaze
to the clock display.

Twenty-five minutes past seven.

She swallowed the emotions swelling at the
back of her throat. Only five minutes to go.

Beneath the exquisite silk dress, which had
been delivered to her hotel room along with
the handwritten note that morning, Carrie's
heart raged. Damon was *all* she had been able
to think about since their parting the previous night. She had lain in bed, giddily awake,
recalling every intimate detail about him.
His mesmerising gold-ringed coffee-brown
gaze. The low, elegant timbre of his voice

that had brushed across her senses like velvet. His crisp evergreen scent that had shot straight through her when he'd moved in close to place that lingering goodnight kiss on her cheek, just a whisper from her lips.

Picturing him at that very moment, awaiting her arrival at a grand, ancient chateau in Paris, one of the most magical cities in the world, was making her blood rush and her heart skip several of its frantic, fevered beats. Yet as she turned to make a final check of her appearance in the full-length mirror and met her reflection, it was a set of dark green eyes glittering with trepidation that stared back at her.

Because there was one other thing about Damon that had kept her wide awake.

His name.

Meyer. Damon Meyer.

A name she was heartbreakingly familiar with.

Because as a young boy Damon had been forced to endure the loss of his father due to the actions of *her* father.

The Meyer-Randolph Scandal, as the shocking events had been dubbed by the media, had seen their fathers' prolific professional partnership end in tragedy when her father's seismic betrayal had unleashed a fury that had cost Jacob Meyer his life. And before the attraction between them went any further Carrie knew she needed to tell Damon exactly who she was.

The fact that she was estranged from her father didn't matter. Although she'd been raised by her mother, far away from her father's influence, and had never been part of the family empire, *and* had long ago divested herself of the name she'd been born with, Sterling Randolph was still her father. And Carrie was always honest. After the way Nate had deceived her, with every word and every look, honesty was of unparalleled importance to her—to always be truthful and to always receive the truth in return.

But the thought of how Damon would react to the truth unleashed a swarm of butterflies as large as bats in her chest. There was every chance that he would walk away without a single second's hesitation, because whilst the person responsible for Jacob's death had been arrested and convicted, in Damon's eyes her father was the real culprit.

Carrie knew he wasn't innocent. Her father's actions had caused a lot of pain, and Carrie would live for ever with the debilitating panic attacks that had been triggered by the media hounding they'd endured in the wake of the scandal, but she'd never considered him entirely responsible, and she hadn't expected Damon would either.

But when her curiosity about him had prompted an online search, amongst the thousands upon thousands of hits that Damon's name had generated—detailing everything from his gorgeous female companions to his celebrity friends and the homes he owned across five continents—she had seen how wrong she was. Every bit of the animosity Damon felt for her father was there in black and white.

His distaste for his business practices. His frustration that Sterling had escaped from the scandal unscathed, as well as his certainty that he was solely to blame for it all.

As Carrie had read, her stomach had twisted into tighter and tighter knots—because had he known who she was the previous night, she knew Damon would not have looked her way.

But he had…and it had been wonderful and exhilarating.

It had been such a long time since Carrie had felt even the tiniest shimmer of attraction for a member of the opposite sex. No man she'd met had come close to penetrating the fear and mistrust that Nate's deception had burdened her with. But that had changed last night with Damon.

A single searing look and slow half-smile from him had jolted her as if she'd been shocked with electricity, setting her heart alight and infusing her blood with streaks of fire. He'd introduced himself and held out his hand, and though the name had sent a shocked charge zipping along her veins, the warmth that had spread to the rest of her body when his long fingers had closed around hers had pushed the significance of his identity entirely from her mind.

Because suddenly every inch of her had been tingling with a sensitivity she instinctively knew could only be soothed by him.

As easily and as quickly as that she had been lost. Except it had felt as if she was found.

A warm shiver danced down Carrie's spine as the feelings she'd been flooded with the previous night rushed back to her. And even as sparks of anxiety continued to flash in her eyes like warning lights she crossed to the door, hoping with all her heart that now he'd found her Damon would want to keep her, even after she told him who she was.

Damon Meyer resisted the urge to glance again at his watch. Carrie was late, and a voice in his head was starting to question if she was going to show up at all—a voice he quickly silenced with the assurance that such a rejection was unlikely.

Every signal she'd transmitted the previous night had said that she wanted to see him again and continue what had been started. He'd read it in the reluctance of her gaze to part with his, and in the tremor of desire that had rippled through her when he'd kissed her goodnight, their lips tantalisingly close to touching. He'd had to draw on all his control not to pull her tight against him and claim her as his own then and there!

But tonight he was giving himself permission to act on those heady impulses—provided that was Carrie's wish too.

It wouldn't be anything more than a fleeting affair. Damon had neither the time nor the energy to devote to a real relationship. He'd long ago committed himself, heart and soul, to his revenge against Sterling Randolph, and he would not stray from that path until Randolph had paid for putting his father in an early grave.

That score, however, was getting closer to being settled. And once the Caldwell deal was his he'd have done it. But that was business, and for the evening ahead he wanted to focus solely on pleasure…

The hum of conversation surrounding him fell away and all thought vanished from his mind as Damon's gaze zeroed in on the striking figure just arriving. His heart started to pound with an unfamiliar tempo, and as Carrie's searching eyes found his, the same bolt of attraction that had drawn them together the previous evening flashed through Damon, white-hot and stronger than anything he had ever experienced.

'Excuse me,' Damon said to his guests, unbothered by their startled surprise as he abruptly exited mid-conversation.

Never taking his eyes off Carrie, he cut a path through the growing number of guests to where she was on the upper terrace. Coming to a stop before her, he could only stare, a hot feeling stirring low in his stomach, as his eyes were drawn to all the mesmerising ways the magenta silk kissed the gentle curves of her body.

The moment Damon had seen that dress he'd known that he wanted to see Carrie in it. The outfit she'd worn the night before had been stylish, but muted. The dark colour and the modest design had flattered her body—there had been no doubt about that, given the way *his* body had reacted to her in it—but it had been designed to allow the wearer to blend in, and some innate inner sense told him that was exactly why she had selected it.

His choice of gown, however, allowed for no such hiding. Whilst the dress hinted at more skin than it actually revealed, with its deep neckline and invisible leg slit, it was a daring cut, and with her silken fall of raven hair hanging straight and sleek over her narrow shoulders and down her back, she looked sensational. The lightest dusting of smoky shadow enhanced her already beautifully wide eyes, making them look even bigger and brighter. And her lips…*those lips*.

Damon wanted to kiss her. In that second it was the sole thought in his mind. He wanted to banish the space between their bodies, draw her into his arms, hold her against the heat of his body and slant his mouth over hers, finally know the feel and taste of her.

Dazed by the force of his wanting, Damon took a second longer than necessary to locate his voice. 'You look even more incredible than I thought you would,' he said, his voice roughened with a craving that only deepened as his words caused a rosy blush to unfurl across her cheekbones.

'So do you,' Carrie replied, although her exquisite olive-green eyes had yet to break the searing connection of their gazes to take in the flawlessly fitted black suit and pristine white shirt he wore. 'And the chateau is spectacular. I've never seen anything like it.'

'Thank you,' he replied, though he did not care one iota about the chateau in that moment. Only her.

It had been only twenty-four hours since he'd met Carrie, and he had spent no more than a handful of those hours with her, yet to Damon it seemed as though he'd been waiting to touch her for ever. The ache to feel her melt beneath him was deep and visceral, sending heat rushing through his blood and tightening his groin.

His attention was so fixed on her that it only took a second for him to spot the pulse hammering in the sweet hollow of her neck. A rapid sweep of his eyes revealed even more signs of nervousness—the firm way her lips were pressed together, the white-knuckled curl of her fingers around her clutch bag. He didn't want her to feel anything in the slightest bit negative, but he could understand how the extravagance of this evening might be overwhelming to a girl from a small, close-knit community in Santa Barbara.

Everything about the evening was overwhelming: the sprawling chateau designed to resemble a fairy-tale castle, the grandeur of the party upon which no expense had been spared, the few hundred personally selected guests, each of them demonstrating their precocious wealth in the diamonds, rubies and emeralds that glittered around their throats and on their ears and fingers.

And most overwhelming of all was the attraction that held them both in its thrall. Even Damon was finding the ferocity of their chemistry intense.

He took a step forward, banishing the distance between them. He saw the tremble that ran over her shoulders as he breached her personal space and her long dark lashes lowered, shielding the uncertain flicker of her eyes.

'I'm glad you're here,' he said, his voice low and soft. Reassuring.

Carrie emitted a shaky breath. 'I...'

He couldn't stand her lowered gaze. Gently he placed a finger under her chin and tilted her head up, so the full force of her eyes once again rested on him, and as she read whatever emotion it was he could feel burning through him, the conflict and anxiety she was battling seemed to ebb away. 'So am I,' she responded softly. 'I'm happy I got the chance to see you again.'

'Did you really think I wouldn't do everything in my power to make sure we had that chance?' he questioned smilingly, feeling much more at ease as he stood close enough to feel the heat from her body. 'In the interest of full and forthright disclosure, I have spent all day unable to think of little else other than seeing you tonight.'

'I've been thinking a lot about you too.'

'Good,' he responded, and felt a violent kind of euphoria barrelling though him that she was just as enthralled as he was.

But then emotions that didn't stay long enough for him to discern flittered across her expression, and she pulled in a quivering breath. 'But there is something I should mention before we…before this…'

From the corner of his eye Damon detected the multitude of glances being directed their way. Attention was nothing new to him. From the moment of his first architectural success he'd been the focus of countless profiles and interviews, attracting attention for being his father's son and for the unexpected sensation caused by his work. From then his profile had exploded.

Fame had never been something he craved, but he'd quickly realised it could be to his advantage. The bigger his profile, the more publicity his takedown of Randolph would attract—and he wanted the whole world to witness his downfall! So he smiled and waved, consented to interviews and accepted invitations to the biggest dates in the social calendar. And as all that attention turned him into a figure with even more renown than his father, it became impossible for him to attend an event without at least a dozen strangers making a beeline for him, eager to see him and be seen with him.

And, judging by the hungry looks from some of those who'd been lucky enough to make it onto the exclusive guest list, tonight would be no different.

But Carrie was also drawing a fair amount of speculation, which was no surprise given how sensational she looked, and he estimated it would be only another ninety seconds before they were interrupted. That was the last thing he wanted. He was in no mood to share.

'Let's take a walk,' he interrupted, sliding a hand to her lower back to guide her away from the curiosity of the crowds. 'I'll show you the chateau.'

'Can it wait a second? I really do need to say something,' she said, as he extracted a key from the inner pocket of his jacket and fitted it into a lock, pushing open a tall, panelled door and gesturing her inside.

'We can talk inside.'

Carrie looked between him and the open door uneasily. 'Are you sure this is allowed?'

He lifted his shoulders in an unconcerned shrug. 'I have the keys. I'm the architect. I think we can get away with it.'

'I don't want to get you in any trouble.'

Damon couldn't help but smile. He was already in deep trouble where she was concerned.

'It'll be fine,' he assured her. 'Besides, what is the point of knowing the architect if you don't get a private tour?' He gestured for her to step inside. 'Now, what was it you needed to tell me?'

But Carrie wasn't listening to him. She had fallen still, admiring the large room they were in, her eyes wide and her lips parted in awe-struck wonderment.

'Damon, this is beautiful,' she breathed, her eyes hungrily taking in the room from floor to ceiling, slowing over all the intricate detail. 'It's like stepping back to a different time.'

'The brief the owner gave me was to restore it to its former glory with just a few contemporary touches.

'The detail is incredible. *All* of it is incredible,' she said.

Her unfiltered awe made his achievement seem even greater. Bigger than when he had declared the project complete. And as she continued to admire the room Damon was interested only in admiring her: the shape of her body, her graceful movements, the glow the low lighting cast across her smooth skin.

'Is the owner going to live here?'

'I'm not sure. Perhaps. He's also considering utilising it as an investment, renting it out for events. He's hosting his daughter's wedding here in a few months. I imagine he'll decide after that.'

'It's a spectacular place for a wedding.' Carrie turned to him, her eyes lively and curious. 'Was it projects like this that made you want to be an architect?'

Unhappy with how far away she had strayed from him, Damon took the opportunity to close the space between them as he answered her question. 'Not especially, no. Buildings like this are special, and I enjoy getting to work on them, but no. I…erm… I wanted to be an architect because my dad was one.'

He had admitted that a hundred times before, but saying it to Carrie felt different somehow, as if he was placing an old key in a different lock, opening up something new. He hesitated, feeling that sense generating a faint pulse of unease, but then he caught the way she was regarding him from her rounded beautiful eyes and it was a look that was utterly compelling. A look that made him feel that there was no place to hide. Or, even more poignantly, no *need* to hide.

'He specialised in urban planning, development and regeneration, working a lot with local governments, but he was an architect first and foremost. He loved buildings—especially old grand ones like this, with a rich and proud history. He liked delving into the story of a building and using that to guide his designs. He just loved building things in a way that was infectious. So I did too. He took me to every site he worked on…walked me through the structure, showed me the plans and asked what I thought. It was our father-son thing. I once told him I thought a wall was in the wrong place. He went back to the plans and changed the design, then told me I was a natural, maybe even better than him. And he was the best. It was never really a decision to choose the same career. I always knew I wanted to be just like him. And after he died, I was even more set on following in his footsteps,' he admitted, realising as he said the words how much truth they carried.

Damon had allowed himself to believe that it was his thirst for revenge that had been the strongest hand in guiding his future and setting him on the path he'd hurtled along—and, yes, it was revenge that dictated which projects he sought and which contacts he prioritised. But he had been born to be an architect. It was in his blood. His heart.

Somewhere along the way he had forgotten that—a fact that disconcerted him nearly as much as the amount of personal information he'd just divulged.

'How old were you? When he died?' Carrie asked.

Her whole expression had changed, and she was watching him with a tentativeness he usually found offensive. He was not fragile. He was not in pain. His father's death had broken his heart and broken up his family, but it had not broken *him*. It had made him strong, purposeful.

'I was twelve.' Damon kept his face blank, his body straight and tall, even as the excruciating memory forced its way to the surface. The crowds. The anger. The cameras there to capture it all. And then the gunshot.

He heard it as if he was there again in that very moment. He could taste the bitter adrenaline in his mouth, feel the terrified thuds of his heart as he lay on the ground, not knowing what was happening. And then the scream, ripping from his throat when he realised exactly what had happened.

Carrie's eyes glistened with the sudden gathering of moisture and she shook her head. 'I'm so sorry, Damon.'

And he knew she really was. It was unnerving, how her heartfelt sympathy made his insides twist. He was used to the platitude, and the faux sympathy with which it was usually delivered, but from Carrie it was genuine. He could hear it in her words. See it in her eyes. She knew his pain even as he concealed it, even as he fought it. She felt it as though she was holding his heart in her hands and could see how it had been ravaged by that single moment in time.

And yet that was not possible, because he did not give his heart away.

'Thank you.'

And suddenly the despised grief was upon him again, burning the backs of his eyes and obstructing his throat. Making spasms ripple across his chest like tremors of an earthquake. Threatening to bring him collapsing in on himself. The breath-stealing pain advanced as if the loss had happened only yesterday.

Damon turned away, outraged by the upwelling of unwanted sorrow. It was a wasteful, weak emotion. And pain was futile, a burden to his soul. It was for that reason he had skipped right past pain and settled happily into a state of anger. Anger was good. It instigated purpose and action. Anger was his daily fuel.

He concentrated on pulling the face of Sterling Randolph into his mind, the memory of his arrogance and the smugness of his family, wanting to feel the rage those images evoked, wanting it to rise up and smother the anguish racking his heart. But before he could summon any picture of his enemy he felt the warmth of a body, a hand curling around his bicep. Within seconds her gentle touch was bringing him back, pulling him from the edge of that black despair. Her deep green eyes were the first thing he saw, and it was their brightness he clung to until the lash of pain began to subside, to the point where he no longer needed to hold his breath.

Carrie's lips parted, as though she was about to offer words of solace, but instead she gave a small shake of her head. There were no words. Damon knew that already. No words capable of adequately sympathising over how the squeeze of that trigger had changed his life—obliterating his present, casting his future into the wind, altering his landscape of family and love and trust for ever. But the fact that she understood that, too, created a connection that anchored him deeper than what he already felt for her. It hitched in his chest, hooked around his heart.

And just her standing beside him was enough. Her hand against his arm. Her sorrowful gaze reaching into his. He didn't feel the pain. He didn't need the anger. All he needed was her.

Turning his face, he grazed her wrist with his mouth and saw the shudder that shimmied through her. It drew a smile across his lips, as did the beam of hunger that flared in her eyes.

Her lips called to him again. Everything about her called to him. But there was something extra-special about her mouth that was driving him past the point of desperation. The simple act of looking at her, seeing her clear olive-green gaze blinking with a growing dazedness, was stirring his erection, and he knew he could not hold out much longer against this connection zinging between them. Nor did he wish to.

The sudden sound of music floating into the room had Carrie angling her head with curiosity.

'It's coming from the ballroom,' he told her.

Her eyebrows arched, her smile full of wonder. 'There's a ballroom?'

He led her across the gleaming white marbled floor of the hall, opulent with its double staircase coming down in curved arms of intricately designed wrought-iron and its spectacular antique chandelier high above them, and into the ballroom.

The room was as high as it was wide, with intricate gold leaf patterning the walls, another sparkling chandelier hanging from the high ceiling and numerous sets of French doors leading to fairy-lit gardens beyond.

Carrie slipped her hand from his and walked into the middle of the room, spinning on the spot as she absorbed the fairy-tale grandeur. 'This is magical. I didn't think anything like this existed outside of films or… you know, royal palaces.'

She was a romantic. He would have assumed so anyway, but now he could see it in the dreaminess of her expression, in her imagining of a love story unfolding in the very setting they were stood in.

With a gesture of his hand Damon gestured to the practising orchestra to start playing again and walked towards Carrie, his arms catching her as she turned to face him. Before she could react, he pulled her in snug against his body, his right arm curling around her waist, and with her smile of delight still floating on her lips he started to move her across the floor.

'What are you doing?' She laughed, self-conscious colour staining her cheeks.

'Dancing with you.'

He hadn't planned it. It had been a complete spur-of-the-moment decision based on her obvious pleasure and his burning desire to have her in his arms and against his body. And this was something he could give her—a night that very few other men on the planet could offer. He would not stay in her life beyond these few hours and days, but he could ensure she would never forget the time they had together.

'Is that a problem?'

The laughter in her expression faded, turning it serious. 'No.'

There was an intimacy to their movements that he had not expected to come from something as simple as dancing, but Damon found he liked it. At least he liked dancing with her.

Pulling her in closer, he splayed his fingers over the lowest point of her back until she was pressed gloriously against the hot muscled wall of his chest. He heard her sudden intake of breath and kept moving to the gentle music. He was aware of every line of her body, every shaky breath she was taking, and every staccato beat of her heart.

Not for one second did their gazes stray from each other, and as the music built towards its crescendo Damon dipped her, his arm supporting her back as he tilted her downwards, his head following to press a kiss to the hollow beneath her chin, his lips brushing against a flickering pulse-point.

When he brought her back upright Carrie's eyes were glazed with the same need that was pounding through his blood. He didn't remove his arms from around her, and nor did she make any attempt to retreat from him. Her palms were resting lightly against his chest and her lips parted with anticipation.

Damon didn't really know why he was waiting…only that looking into her mesmerising eyes held an eroticism of its own, seeing her hunger as well as his own reflected back at him. Her breathing hitched even higher, and as her eyes dropped tellingly to his mouth he lowered his face and grazed his lips against hers for the barest second. It was just a taste, but it was long enough for him to know that she was paradise.

'Damon. Excellent. I've been looking for you.'

The voice rang through the large, empty room, causing Carrie to jump guiltily free of his arms. Damon turned his head to see the owner of the chateau coming to a hasty stop as he looked between him and Carrie, belatedly realising that he had interrupted.

Damon cleared his throat, smoothing over the moment of unease. 'Jean-Pierre, this is Carrie Miller. Carrie, this is the chateau's owner—Jean-Pierre Valdon.'

'It's a pleasure to meet you, Mademoiselle Miller,' Jean-Pierre murmured, a smile playing about his lips as he bowed his head in Carrie's direction.

'Likewise. And congratulations. The chateau and everything about tonight is incredible. I'll let you two talk.'

Damon began to protest, turning to Carrie with a frown and tightening his hold on her fingers, but she shook her head lightly.

'It's fine. I could use some air anyway.' She squeezed his fingers and sent him an uneven smile. 'I'll catch up with you outside.'

Before he could react she was hurrying from the ballroom, and only his eyes were able to follow her.

Oh, God, what had she done? What had she *done*?

Sneaking off with him. Letting him confide in her his pain over his father. And then dancing with him. *Kissing* him.

Carrie's head felt on the cusp of explosion, with her heart launching itself against her ribs over and over again as she pressed down on the handle of every door she could find until one opened and she tumbled out into the garden and clean night air washed over her, blessedly cool against her burning skin.

She was supposed to have told him the truth the second she arrived—told him exactly who she was. That had been her intention. She'd rehearsed the words in her head, she'd had them ready, but then...

Then their eyes had met in a way she'd thought could only happen in fairy-stories. And he had looked at her with a glowing appreciation that had made her dizzy, and she had known that he had been seeing *her*, Carrie Miller, the woman she was. Not her name, not her father's wealth and influence, but *her*. And he had touched her. It had been a tiny, insignificant press of his finger to her chin, but that small, single moment of connection had been so potent that she had almost gone up into flames.

Still, she'd tried. Or at least she thought she had—it was all a bit fuzzy. But then he'd taken her hand and led her into the house and...

It had all just been so overwhelming.

He was overwhelming. And so was the connection between them. Too overwhelming for Carrie, in all her inexperience, to know how to handle.

She'd felt attraction before, or so she had believed. Even after discovering that Nate had not been what he'd seemed, that their relationship had not been at all what she had thought, Carrie had recognised that she'd played right into his hands by being swept off her feet by his traditional handsomeness.

But none of the time she'd spent with Nate had contained the spectacular sizzling electricity of the past hour. Her heart had never beaten so keenly in his company, and her body had never been so attuned to his hands and his eyes, so in thrall to him the way she was to Damon.

Whatever it was that she'd felt for Nate had been a pale and weak prologue.

This, with Damon, was attraction. Passion. Heat.

This, with Damon, was overwhelmingly, thrillingly, terrifyingly real.

So real it obliterated all else—like the truth she needed to tell him. And she could hardly go back and tell him now, could she?

Not after willingly pressing her body up against his and thrumming with a need that his very masculine touch promised to assuage.

Not after letting him reveal to her the depth of his pain over the loss of his father.

A sob of anguish rose in her throat.

When the conversation had turned towards Damon's father her heart had vaulted out of her chest. It had been such an unguarded moment on his part, a raw glimpse of his hurt, and what made Carrie feel absolutely wretched was the sense that Damon didn't lift that curtain very often. But he had let her peek behind it and see his vulnerability, all the while unaware that she was the daughter of the man whose betrayal had kick-started the tragedy.

If he learned who she was now, he would surely consider it a deception of the cruellest kind. And she wouldn't blame him.

She had deceived him. She hadn't told the truth.

With agonising tears pressing against the backs of her eyes, Carrie knew there was only one thing she could do now—leave.

Allowing herself no time to change her mind, and hoping that if she moved quickly enough she could slip away undetected whilst Damon was still engaged in his conversation, she began to move through the shadows of the garden, hurriedly slipping along the pathways bordered by manicured shrubs and trees.

'Carrie!'

She heard the shout of her name over the cacophony of the party, but she kept moving her feet, kept her eyes forward though her heart jolted. She would be able to go faster if she wasn't navigating the ground in five-inch heels, but to stop and take her shoes off would take too much time, and right now she just needed to get away without facing Damon.

Relief raced through her as she realised she was drawing near to a set of steps that would take her to an exit point, but then a figure leapt down in front of her, landing with an agile crouch before straightening to his impeccable full height.

'Damon!' Carrie gasped, looking from him up to the level he had jumped from and feeling her heart catch. 'Are you crazy? You could have broken something,' she admonished, whilst her eyes tracked quickly over his athletic body, checking for any sign of injury.

He dismissed her concern with a careless slice of his hand through the air, surveying her with dark-eyed bewilderment. 'Where are you going?'

'I have a…' But a suitable fib would not

rise to her lips and she ended up shaking her head. 'I need to leave.'

'Are you unwell?' His eyes scanned her face, seeking a clue as to what had changed in the space of a few minutes. 'Has something happened?'

'No. I just… I can't stay.'

He said nothing, but his penetrating stare seemed to reach inside her and grasp at her heart, and with that single look the emotion filling up her body grew bigger somehow, and much less easy to contain.

Before she could stop them, words were tumbling from her lips. 'I shouldn't have come here tonight, Damon, okay? I shouldn't have… I… I'm sorry, but this was a mistake. And now I need to leave.'

Ignoring the shadow that scudded across his expression like a cloud, Carrie moved to sidestep him. But Damon anticipated her evasion and moved quickly, blocking her path with an outstretched arm.

She froze, her heart flailing as she realised she was effectively trapped.

'There is someone else?' he asked roughly, his warm and soft breath hitting the sensitive skin of her ear and making her think of that briefest of kisses.

It had been no more than a graze, but it had

sent feeling trickling all the way down to the tops of her toes and the tips of her fingers. And she wanted to experience it all over again.

'No.' She wished it was that simple. 'But that doesn't change anything.'

She summoned just enough courage to raise her face and meet his gaze, and did her best to inject into her voice a conviction that she didn't feel.

'Whatever this is between us, it can't happen. It can't go beyond now, tonight. It should never have started in the first place. So, please, just let me go.'

'No,' he answered, with so much determined power surging into his eyes it was like a fireworks display. 'Not until you give me the real reason you're running away from this.'

CHAPTER TWO

THIS WAS IT THEN, Carrie thought, feeling unsteady as Damon's demand for an answer hung in the taut air between them. The perfect moment to tell him.

She gathered a breath, already knowing what she needed to say.

My father is Sterling Randolph.

That was it. Five small words.

Yet as hard as she tried she couldn't make the words form. Couldn't make her lips move. Because she knew that once she spoke those words aloud to him there could be no going back, and she was terrified of seeing that beautiful gaze, now fixed on her with such heat and passion, turn arctic with the loathing that she knew ran through his veins.

Because without a shadow of doubt she knew that once he learned who her father was her name would, yet again, be the only thing about her that mattered.

It had been all that had mattered to her high school friends, who had stopped talking to her because her father had killed a man. It had been all that had mattered to Nate, who hadn't wanted her as much as he had wanted to ingratiate himself with her father and snag himself a little corner of the Randolph empire. And it had been all that had mattered when she had been headhunted for the dream job of pastry chef at a new Parisian restaurant.

She had been so stupidly excited, so proud of the offer and the hard work and skill that she thought had got her noticed so quickly, but they had only wanted her in order to forge a connection with her father, to invite his patronage, perhaps even his investment.

Discovering that had crushed her.

Eventually she had abandoned her father's name for good. She had returned to Santa Barbara to pull the broken pieces of herself back together and had rebuilt herself as Carrie Miller, creating a life and a business without the weight that accompanied her globally recognisable surname.

It was the best thing she had ever done. Not only did her anonymity feel like a shield against any repeat of the frenzied media hounding that had followed her family and traumatised her as a little girl, it also gave her the luxury of knowing that all her success these past few years was her own, earned by hard work, dedication and skill.

That was all she wanted—to be recognised and treated as her own person, to be judged on her own merits and mistakes, to be accepted and loved for the person she was and not the name she bore.

But, with the past being what it was, would Damon really be able to do that when he was still in so much agony over his father's death?

Would he be able to see her as Carrie Miller and nothing more?

'It's complicated, Damon,' she said finally, trying to contend with the disappointment crashing through her that she ultimately wasn't brave enough to take that chance. 'You just need to trust me. It is better for both of us if this begins and ends right now.'

Displeasure had Damon's jaw tightening, and Carrie braced herself for a further demonstration of truculence, but instead his arm curled around her waist, and before she knew what was happening he had drawn her flush against his hard body and his mouth had come sweeping down against hers.

The sensation of his firm lips moving with slow sensuality against hers had her eyes fluttering closed, and as the sharp sweetness of the kiss pierced all Carrie's levels of resistance her body softened with a surrender she had thought it was impossible for her to feel.

For the last five years the thought of being touched by another man had consumed Carrie with fear and anxiety. The memory of how each and every one of Nate's caresses had been a lie, a mere tool to draw her in and use her for his own ends, had caused her to retreat from whatever small moments of attraction she'd felt and from any physical contact with the opposite sex. But with Damon she was aware of only the heat between them, so hot it burnt away all else, leaving no oxygen for doubts to feed on. She could only feel the rightness of his caresses, could only think of having more—more of his mouth, more of his hands on her body. More and more and more.

'Say that again,' Damon murmured against her lips. 'Now you know how I taste, tell me again that it's better to end this now.'

Carrie couldn't. All she could do was stare at him, dazed and amazed and silent. She hadn't known it was possible for a kiss to be so compelling, to leave her feeling so replete and yet hungry for more at the same time.

With her legs threatening to turn into liquid as the impassioned heat of their kiss continued to burn through her, Carrie curled the hands resting against his strong chest around the lapels of his jacket as her quivering body half collapsed against his. It was a mistake, but one she didn't recognise until it was too late…until she was achingly aware of every solid line and ridge of his body and the awesome power contained beneath the suavely dressed surface and the gentlemanly veneer it projected.

The thrumming she could feel beneath her hands and the steely press of his erection left her in no doubt that beneath the gentleman was a *man*. A hot-blooded man who hungered and craved, who sought and took. Who knew how to use his body to drive a woman wild.

As though to prove that very point, Damon lifted a hand to her face and trailed his fingers lightly across her cheekbone. 'You said this can't go beyond tonight…but what about tonight? Can we have that?'

The question was unexpected, and Carrie blinked with surprise. Damon's eyes held a gleam…a look that sent a thousand shivers skittering across her bare shoulders and had feeling pulsing all over her body. She understood what he was asking, what he was proposing. One night together. No questions asked, no answers needed. A continuation of what they had already started.

She should say no. She knew that. That was the smart thing to do. The *right* thing to do. But the voice urging that course of action had become very quiet, almost muted by the force of that kiss and by her need for this one man that was building with every passing second, blooming into something larger and stronger every time he touched her.

And Carrie knew in that second that there was only one answer she could give to his question. It was not a choice. It was not a decision. It was a need—an imperative. And it had been from the first moment their eyes had locked.

One night with him. That was all. And then she would walk away, as she already should have done.

'Yes, we can have tonight,' she answered, barely able to hear her voice over the riotous beats of the heart.

'Then if that's all we have, let's not waste it. Let's go somewhere. Just you and me.'

'But the party....' Carrie began, looking up to where music and chatter and laughter drifted down to them.

'Forget about the party. I don't need to be here. It's just a chance for Jean-Pierre to show off his chateau. I would rather be with you.'

He wound his fingers through hers, then

brought their intertwined hands to brush against his lips. And it was only the lightest press of his mouth, but it completely undid the last bonds holding her together.

'Then let's go,' she said, and smiled before she could think twice.

Damon took her to his penthouse. It was just off the Champs-Elysées, nestled within the architectural beauty and all-round luxury of the city's Golden Triangle. From the large terrace it offered spectacular midnight views across the whole city. With one sweep of her eyes Carrie could look from the Eiffel Tower to the Sacré-Coeur Basilica to the American Cathedral and the Pantheon.

She did her best to concentrate on the breathtaking sight, but she was too aware of the nerves that had her stomach swooping and the whirring of too many thoughts in her head. Doubts and questions over what she was doing…what she was thinking. *If* she was thinking.

She knew she had not yet passed the point of no return. She could change her mind and leave, let the memory of Damon fade until it was as if meeting him again had never happened. But then she heard footsteps behind her, and as she looked over her shoulder her eyes crashed into Damon's, that sinfully slow smile worked its way across his lips, and her head fell silent. The flutters in her chest disappeared. Even her stomach settled. And there was only a peaceful kind of certainty that, even though it was a tangled mess, and even though Damon with his string of previous girlfriends and very public lifestyle was entirely the wrong man to be taking this chance with, she was exactly where she needed to be. Where she should be.

As he arrived at her side, Damon held out a glass of champagne. 'For you.'

'Thank you.'

'I ordered us some food. It shouldn't take long to be delivered.'

Silken heat kissed her skin as he settled himself beside her and he, too, fixed his attention on the illuminated cityscape spread out before them.

'I always forget how incredible it is looking out over this city at night. Living here, I take it for granted, I suppose.'

'How long have you lived here?'

'Not long.'

He set down his champagne glass and shrugged out of his jacket, pulling apart the top few buttons of his shirt with an easy flick of his fingers before doing the same to the cuffs, and then pushing them up his forearms in a mesmerising motion that captivated her attention.

'I bought it when I was hired to work on the chateau. I didn't want to be living in hotels. But I wouldn't say I've *lived* here. More like crashed when I wasn't working.'

An image of him tumbling into bed exploded in her mind, sending waves of heat crashing through her and she had to avert her eyes.

'You mentioned that you lived in Paris too?' he said.

'Yes. A couple of years ago. I came here for cookery school and stayed about eight months.'

'You weren't tempted to stay longer?' he asked with an easy smile. 'Open a little patisserie on the Left Bank? Enjoy this view every day?'

'I was tempted—although where I lived, I did not have a view like this.'

Her father had not supported her ambition to cook, but he had offered up a penthouse for her to live in—an offer that Carrie had refused. After witnessing his chilling ruthlessness for herself, and having her eyes yanked open to see how little she actually mattered to him, she hadn't wanted to take *anything* from him.

'But I'm not sure I could really imagine

being so far away from my family, unable to see them whenever I wanted. Plus…'

'Plus…?' he probed when she stalled.

'Plus, one of the reasons I came to Paris in the first place was to get away,' she continued with care, not wanting to say too much and yet wanting him to understand. 'To start over and be someone else. But I learned it's not that easy to do.'

She was staring straight ahead, but Carrie felt his gaze closing around her. Surveying. Deducing and then understanding.

'Someone hurt you?'

'Yes.'

But Carrie still didn't know who had hurt her more—Nate or her father—and which one she had been running from.

All she'd known at the time was that she hadn't wanted to be Carrie Randolph any more. The thought of spending one more day walking around with that target on her back had been unbearable. But she had been naïve, thinking she could leave her identity behind. That she could jet off to Paris, change her name, live in a tiny attic apartment and simply stop being a Randolph.

Her mother had tried to warn her, but she had been too desperate to hear her, and she'd had to learn the hard way that she couldn't change anything by trying to outrun it. All she'd ended up doing was inviting more hurt.

But she did not want to think about any of that with Damon. She didn't want her father or the past intruding on the happiness she felt with him. She just wanted to be simple Carrie Miller from Santa Barbara. And yet once again the complication and deceit had her insides twisting, as if poison was slithering through her bloodstream.

'All I will say is that he was obviously exceedingly stupid. And I suggest we don't waste a second talking about him,' he proposed, with a sinfully quick quirk of his lips.

Whether it was his words or the tantalising flash of his sexy smile, Carrie didn't know, but emotion pulsed in the air between them and she could have sworn she felt the ground beneath her feet actually shift. She could see that Damon felt it, too, but before she was even sure how to respond to the sudden flare of sensation Damon already was, extracting her glass from her suddenly limp hand and placing it on the table behind him.

'Maybe we shouldn't waste a second talking at all.'

He moved in even closer and slid his strong hands around her waist, lowering his mouth to hers slowly…slowly enough for her to stop him if she wanted. But Carrie didn't want to.

The languid kiss delivered a wicked kind of pleasure. It was thorough and purposeful, each slide of his lips telling her how much he wanted her, and knowing that it was just about *her*, the woman, and not the name or the opportunity, sent its effect spiralling even deeper into her core.

His hands moved up her back in a possessive slide, tunnelling into the long lengths of her hair as he slanted his mouth to both offer and take more. Her mouth opened beneath his, an invitation for the advent of his tongue which he accepted without hesitation. And his tongue playing against hers sent tendrils of electric sensation shooting in all directions, pressing her close to melting point.

She had not thought it a foregone conclusion that she would spend the night with him, but in that instant she knew there could be no other. They had set something alight that needed to burn itself out. Names, the past— all of it was suddenly irrelevant. All that mattered was that there was him and there was her. And they had found one another.

They had known each other less than twenty-four hours, and yet Carrie felt she *knew* him. She felt an ease with him that she had not been able to find with any member of the opposite sex since Nate. It felt as if she had been waiting for him, for this moment, this merging, for ever.

Her back bumped against something solid—the wall, she assumed dizzily—and then Damon's lips were running down her neck, his mouth wet and hot against her throat, and his hand was taking advantage of the low cut of her dress to slide inside and cradle her breast. After being untouched for so many years, she felt the skin-to-skin contact as a shock, and a startled gasp spilt from her lips.

Damon stilled. He didn't remove his hand—in fact his fingertips continued to stroke gently up and down the side of her breast—but he drew his head back just enough to allow his eyes to probe hers.

'Too fast? Do you want me to stop?'

'No.' The word fell instantly from her lips, but the shadow of a question lingered in his expression. 'I… It's just been a while since I've been with anyone.'

A beat passed as Damon scrutinised her expression. 'Are you sure this is what you want?' he asked, obviously ready to take a step back even as his eyes burned.

It only made her more certain.

'Yes.' The hand curled around his cheek

guided his mouth back down to hers. 'I want this,' she breathed between light kisses. 'I want *you*.'

I need you, she thought, with even more desperation.

This time when their lips caught Damon emitted a throaty growl and trapped her mouth beneath his, making the stroke of his lips slow, but deep. Carrie felt the effects of it all the way down in her stomach, and even lower in the sudden, insistent thrumming of her pelvis.

As he once again commanded the capitulation of her body, evoking feeling in every single cell she possessed, the fingers curled around her breast slowly began to explore her sensitivity. He brushed the pad of his thumb across her nipple and Carrie moaned into his mouth, bracing herself against the wall as his skilled fingers advanced to pinch and play.

Her hand curled around his shoulder tightened, and his tender exploration of her mouth quickly turned into a heated exchange that his tongue turned into a merciless plunder. Carrie loved every second of it. Being wanted so fiercely. Having someone be this greedy for her.

And then Damon's mouth was replacing his fingers over her breast. The straps of her dress had slipped from her shoulders, revealing her chest to the air, and Damon fastened his lips around her nipple, licking and flicking and sucking in a tantalising rhythm that had her head knocking against the wall and her teeth biting down on her lip, fighting the cries of hunger and madness building in her throat.

She could not fathom the forces he was unleashing within him. Could not understand how his worship of her breast sent her hips arching forward, rocking to a rhythm of their own. Could not figure out how he was making her body *his*. It did not seem plausible that the feelings pulsing through her could be real. Surely such delight, such brazen passion, could only belong in a dream or a fantasy. But she was both awake and alive, and Damon's incredible touch was driving her to places she hadn't known existed.

His mouth came back to hers and her body shaped itself to the hard planes of his. She was aware of the solid ridge of arousal just below his waist. She wanted to feel more of it. All of it. She was nowhere near experienced enough to be sexually confident, and whatever confidence she had once gained had been neutralised by Nate's deception, but in that moment it did not worry her. Everything with Damon was so instinctual—as if her body recognised him, recognised what to do.

Moving on that instinct, she brought her leg up, so their centres rubbed against each other. Damon's body acted on the same impulse, his hands shaping her bottom and pulling her against him, and the lethal rock of his hips against hers had her edging closer and closer to the beckoning oblivion.

They were scorching the air around them. Damon couldn't recall a time when he had been such a slave to his desires. He was controlled by one need and one only—the need for revenge. Very little else registered. Not hunger or thirst or desire. He ate and drank because food and water were placed in front of him. He took a woman to bed as an outlet—for relaxation and release. But he was *hungering* for Carrie. Greedy for her. Not only did he ache to know the secrets of her body, he craved the taste of her as if it had become his one and only life source.

A fire was beating through his blood that had been started by her and could only be quelled by her. He felt the flames of the gathering inferno lick higher as they moved together, his tongue sliding into the sweet cavern of her mouth, and he was unable to stop the thrust of his hips against hers as the honeyed taste of her on his lips made him crazy with longing, urging him to seek and take more of the delights she presented.

His hands slid down her back and curved around her perfectly shaped butt, pulling her in tight to his erection. And, feeling the answering way she moulded herself to him, Damon knew he could not wait another second to see more of her.

Pulling back, he smiled and tugged her along the terrace, reaching behind him to push open the doors that led into the master suite. As soon as she was inside the darkened room his fingers located the discreet fastenings of the dress and undid them. The dress slid down her body to pool at her feet.

Damon would have been lying if he'd claimed he had not envisaged undressing her when he had first pictured her in the dress, but the reality wildly surpassed the fantasy. Now Carrie was bare but for a pink lace thong and the strappy stilettoes and, looking at her, Damon couldn't catch his breath. He wasn't sure he even remembered how to breathe.

Her skin was flushed, glowing, and her eyes were dazzlingly bright. She watched him, watching her, her breathing shallow, and knowing that she wanted this with the same hunger and desperation that was driving him was a satisfaction Damon had not anticipated. Never had he expected to feel a connection so strong to another person. A connection that was so elemental.

She was like heaven on earth. One tiny piece of serenity and bliss amongst the blackness, the desolation and the pain. But if that tragedy, the anger and the pain, had been what he needed to experience in order to be in the time and place to meet her, then Damon felt he could accept that.

For her, everything might have been worth it.

Lowering his head, he pressed teasingly light kisses along her jaw, down her neck to her collarbone, feeding off the gasps of pleasure that broke from her lips. Her whole body quivered and Damon brought his mouth back to hers, swinging her up into his arms to carry her to the large bed.

Instantly he was mourning the loss of her body against his as he stepped back to rid himself of his own clothes. And as he did so he thought of all the ways he wanted to tease and touch her, pleasure her, this woman who had infiltrated his mind, his blood, his dreams, and whose body he could not wait to bury himself inside.

* * *

As she watched him undress, it felt to Carrie as if she was burning up from the inside out. First his shirt was dropped to the floor, revealing a solid expanse of chiselled chest and stomach, and then he was sliding his trousers over his strong legs, leaving only a pair of snug black boxer shorts on his body.

She could not draw her eyes away from his muscled physique and his skin which glowed with a godlike golden sheen. This feeling for him—it went way beyond lust. Deeper than desire. She did not know what to call it, but it had her reaching for him urgently as he came back to the bed, catching him between her open arms as he covered her body with his own. And then he was kissing her again, his hands moving over her with a reverent touch. A touch that was healing.

After the way Nate had used her, seducing her only to advance his own ends, Carrie hadn't been able to think of sex without her stomach churning with nausea. His lies had made it seem tawdry and base. But there was nothing sordid about what was unfolding between her and Damon. Their intimacy felt beautiful. And vital. Nerves fluttered beneath her skin, but they were nothing compared to the feeling of rightness that came from lying beneath him as he grazed his lips down the side of her neck, trailed a hot path between her breasts, down her ribs and over her stomach, seeking lower still.

But just as he was about to guide her legs apart he stopped, glancing up at her, and with a stutter of her heart Carrie realised he was asking her permission to carry on. Moisture sprang into her eyes and she nodded, suddenly aching to feel him touching her *there*, and then, nudging her legs apart, he buried his face in her and pressed an open-mouthed kiss to her delicate feminine folds.

Carrie was already balancing on a knife-edge, and the moment he pressed his tongue and connected it with her hidden core delight screamed through her body. She bucked and twisted beneath him, surrendering control of her own body to the feeling coursing through her, but Damon's firm hand on her stomach held her steady as he worshipped her, kissing and stroking and delving with his tongue, until the shocks shooting through her body became too powerful to resist and she shattered beneath their catastrophic force into a million sparkling pieces.

'Oh, my God… Damon,' she breathed, as the aftershocks zig-zagged up her body with alarming force and he began to kiss his way back up.

He covered her, his erection teasing her wetness. She was still quaking with the ripples of that first orgasm, but the moment she felt him slide against her she was hungering for another, her limbs tensing with anticipation, and she arched against him, unable to help herself, wanting to feel more of what he could do to her.

'Tell me what you want,' he whispered against her ear.

'I want more,' she panted, the words torn from her by a greediness that had his lips curling in a way that told her he had her exactly the way he wanted her. Wet and starving and begging. 'I want all of you.'

He responded with a devastating smile as he reached for a condom from the nightstand. He sheathed himself before positioning himself at her slick entrance, and then he was gently pushing into her, and her muscles were gripping his thick length in ecstatic welcome. A keening cry broke from her lips as with a final thrust he fitted himself fully inside her. He was so hard, his penetration so deep, and the feel of him so overawing, that Carrie struggled to catch her breath. She wanted to savour the moment, but the need for him to take her even further made her impatient.

'Damon…' she ground out, lifting her hips to intensify the feeling building in her.

He sank even deeper. By the strain in his face she knew it cost him to hold himself still as she wriggled beneath him, but then she saw the moment her impatience became his. And then he was moving, retreating from her before driving back inside, his steady tempo intensifying as her hips met and matched his eager thrusts and they raced towards a peak.

She was on the very edge of coming but still holding back when Damon seized her mouth with a bruising kiss and sucked on her lower lip, and Carrie splintered apart in his arms before, with a shout of her name, he surrendered to his own shuddering climax.

Breathless and drained, he fell on top of her, breathing heavily, and Carrie ran a gentle hand up and down his spine whilst his racing heart evened out and the stars behind her eyes faded away. Raising his head with a languid smile, his dark hair messy from all the times she had dragged her fingers through it, he pressed a kiss to her lips, rolling onto his side and pulling her with him.

Just as he was enfolding her in his arms, a knock at the door had him pulling away. 'That will be the food I ordered,' he said, and laughed, sliding out of the bed and grabbing his trousers from the floor. 'Good thing we've worked up an appetite.'

He returned with two bags of food and several plates. They ate out on the terrace, devouring the dishes he had selected, him gloriously bare-chested whilst she wore only his shirt. His lips quirked every time he looked at her, as if he was appreciating the bare legs and the visibility of her breasts beneath the material.

When they were finished, he turned to her. 'Are you tired? Do you want to sleep?'

Under his beautiful gaze, her heart raced, and Carrie felt breathless just looking at him. She wanted to soak up every moment she had with him—wanted to know each and every part of him. If one night was all she could have, then she wanted every single second.

She leaned in, pressing a hand to his chest and bestowing upon him a lingering kiss. 'Let's not waste time sleeping.'

His answering smile told her she had read his mind.

Dawn arrived too soon.

The sharp early-morning light forced Carrie's eyes open and thrust her into painful reality.

Her one night was Damon was over.

An ache spread across her chest and for a small second Carrie considered an alternative scenario—one in which she didn't slink away, but stayed and told him everything. He would be annoyed, of course, but perhaps not as annoyed as she feared. After a moment of absorbing it he would draw her close for a drugging kiss and tell her he didn't care, that she meant more than anything.

But then she remembered his rawness when he had spoken of his father and knew she was withdrawing to one of her fairy-tale fantasies. Allowing herself to believe in it, even for a second, was dangerous. She would only end up hurting even more.

Because the truth was that staying was impossible.

A future between them was impossible.

Beside her, Damon was in a steady sleep, lying on his back with one arm flung behind his head and the sheet riding low over his chiselled stomach. Carrie could feel the heat rising from his body, and the longing to curl up against him, slide her leg across his and rest her head against his strong chest, as she had during the night, reared up within her.

She had to draw on every last drop of her willpower to slip out from beneath the covers and collect her discarded clothes. Once she was back in her dress, carrying her shoes in her hand, she tiptoed to the threshold of the bedroom, unable to resist a last look at him.

He was still sound asleep, his chest rising and falling in a peaceful rhythm. Her eyes throbbed and her throat burned with a new kind of agony. But it was her heart that ached most dreadfully.

She wished it didn't have to be this way… wished so many things were different. But she was a Randolph and he was a Meyer. That simply could not be.

'Goodbye, Damon,' she whispered, turning and leaving before the first tears could fall.

CHAPTER THREE

WEEKS LATER, Carrie was still on Damon's mind.

When he woke on the day of the Caldwell pitch, his first thought was not of the crucial day ahead. It was of Carrie. Exactly as it had been every day since Paris.

Each morning he woke with his naked body tangled in the sheets, dappled with beads of sweat after yet another night spent languishing in a highly sexed dreamscape with Carrie Miller, delighting in the scenarios he hadn't been granted the opportunity to play out in reality.

Because she'd been gone by the time he woke after their night together. Which shouldn't have been a surprise. One night was all she'd been willing to give. One night was all that he had asked for. Usually that was enough. So it really shouldn't have bothered him.

Except waking to cool sheets and an empty

bed *had* bothered him and, contrary to the reassurances he had issued to himself, that the strange feelings of angst over her silent departure were nothing more than a fleeting phenomenon, it was still bothering him.

He didn't understand why. As a general rule he didn't allow himself to form attachments deep enough that ultimately it meant he would miss a person when they were no longer there. And even if that had happened—and that was highly unlikely —he hadn't known Carrie long enough to actually miss her. And yet at times an uncomfortable feeling lodged within his gut, making him feel as though she had somehow infiltrated him emotionally as deeply as he had penetrated her physically.

He didn't like it.

Damon didn't want to be affected by another person. He didn't want his heart, or any other part of him, to be touched, softened. Weakened. Left open and vulnerable. He didn't want to have to feel the agonising pain of a loss that could never be replaced. He didn't want to live day after day with the edges of his heart burning and that inescapable ache threatening to burrow deeper with the slow passing of each second.

With the death of his father and his subsequent abandonment by his mother, Damon had already felt all that too acutely to ever want to relive the experience. And the protective walls he had built around himself were impenetrable.

Which made Carrie's continued lingering in his mind and his errant thoughts of contacting her once he returned to California unfathomable.

And intolerable.

She was nothing to him—nothing other than a beautiful distraction. It was past time he took control of himself.

Today was the day when he would present the final, all-important bid that would seal the Caldwell project and bring him within touching distance of his revenge. The day that he would look back on as the beginning of the end of Sterling Randolph. And that was the only thing he wanted to think about.

After all, he'd been working towards this day for ever. It had taken time to build his business to the point where he could challenge the Randolph Corporation. And it had taken twenty-hour days and endless networking to manoeuvre himself into a position of industry dominance. But he'd done it. He had achieved in ten years what other men had worked thirty years for, and over the past twelve months Damon had begun to shake the industry's confidence in Randolph.

But that wasn't anywhere near enough for him.

He wanted Randolph to feel his success slipping through his fingers as surely as his own father had felt his life slipping away.

And that was where the Caldwell project came in.

The Caldwell Banking Group in London were commissioning a new North American headquarters—a building that was to be a beacon of their global prowess and reputation. Everyone in the world, including Caldwell himself, believed Randolph to be the natural choice to spearhead the project. But for the better part of the past year Damon had been quietly cultivating the Caldwell executives, laying the groundwork to ensure that his bid was the successful one. And when he won it Randolph would be finished, cut down for all the world to witness.

It would not give Damon back any of the things he'd lost, but his father had been a good man, who had only wanted to use his intellect and talent to help people and make the world a better place, so to see the care-less, arrogant man responsible for his death brought to his knees would deliver him an indescribable satisfaction.

When the important work of the day was done, he would find some beauty with whom he could while away the evening hours— someone to shunt Carrie completely from his mind. But for the time being he settled for throwing back the sheets and standing under a cold shower, employing the ruthless discipline he'd spent a lifetime mastering to erase all traces of her.

Because there was no room for her—or anyone—in his head or in his life.

He had one focus, one ambition. And he would not allow anyone to stand in the way of him achieving that.

Because his revenge was what mattered.

It was *all* that mattered.

It was Carrie's day off from the bakery, but she was still working. Sitting back, she looked at the sketch of the five-tier wedding cake she'd been tasked with creating the day before. Pleased with the draft, she set it to the side before bringing up her list of special orders on the computer.

It had grown substantially in the past fortnight, and despite other people's concerns that Carrie was overstretching herself, her heavy workload was exactly what she wanted. And needed. She loved her thriving small business and she loved baking. The latter had been her salvation on a number of occasions, and throwing herself into her work was a key part of her plan to move forward, look only into the future and forget all about Damon Meyer.

Well, not *forget*, exactly, because that was impossible. There could be no forgetting the mind-blowing intimacy they had shared and all the ways he had touched and caressed her body that single night, healing the pieces of her that had still been emotionally black and blue. It was more about keeping her thoughts away from him, keeping herself so busy that she had no time to wonder about him, to wonder if he ever thought about her.

She was just reading through the notes that accompanied the order of a fiftieth birthday cake when a light knock on the window heralded the arrival of her mother.

'I brought you a smoothie, and a little something else,' Prue Miller announced with her usual bright smile as she walked through Carrie's door, setting down her gifts on the table and kissing her daughter's cheek. 'How are you feeling today? Is your stomach any better?'

'A little, yes,' Carrie answered, without taking her eyes off her notes.

'This is beautiful,' Prue said, admiring the cake sketch Carrie had just finished. 'A wedding cake?'

'Yes, I got the order yesterday.' Picking up the smoothie, she took a small sip and was relieved when her stomach didn't instantly heave. 'This is delicious. Thank you.' Reaching for the small bag next to it, she froze when she saw its contents.

A pregnancy test.

Swallowing her shock, but unable to quieten her quickening heart, she lifted her gaze to her mother. Prue was watching her with shrewd eyes, but her expression offered no hint as to what she was thinking.

'How did you know?'

Carrie just about managed to force the question past the tennis-ball-sized lump lodged in her throat.

Prue smiled. 'Because I'm your mother. And that stomach bug you've been suffering from has lingered a little too long for me to believe it really *is* a stomach bug.'

When Carrie made neither a move nor a sound in response, she sighed and retrieved the test from the bag herself, holding it in the air.

'Are you really going to keep me in suspense?'

Carrie trembled as the truth forced its way to her lips. 'I don't need to take the test. I've already done one.'

Her mother moved closer. 'And…?'

Carrie took a fortifying breath, fearful of the look she was about to see in her mother's eyes, and even more terrified of the reality it would become once she said the words aloud.

'It was positive. All four of them were. I'm pregnant.'

In the next second her mother's arms were around her, holding her tightly. 'Sweetheart, are you okay? Why didn't you tell me sooner?'

'I'm fine. I think. Actually, I don't know.'

She sighed, her thoughts and emotions far too jumbled for her to be anywhere close to identifying them.

'Have you given any thought to what you want to do?'

Carrie nodded, meeting her mother's eyes. 'I'm having the baby.'

Prue beamed. 'I'll help in any way I can. The bakery, doctors' appointments—whatever you need.'

'Thanks. But I'm not that far in my thinking yet.'

She was still trying to process the fact that she was pregnant and that it was not happening the way she'd always imagined it would—mainly because the father was a man she'd never anticipated seeing again.

Her mother must have read the struggle in her expression, for she moved beside her, hugging her again. 'It'll be okay, Carrie. You'll figure this out. You're not on your own. And, speaking of that…have you told the father?'

'Not yet.' There was no question in Carrie's mind that she would tell Damon, but she knew she would also have to divulge who she was, and she didn't expect either revelation to be met with delight. 'It's a little complicated.'

'Carrie, I understand the world we live in, and that some relationships happen quickly and are not always long term. I'm not going to judge you for having something casual. And you're certainly entitled to your privacy. So if you're not comfortable telling me, that is fine, but I really think you need to tell *him*.'

'It's not so much the nature of the relationship that makes telling him difficult. At least not only that,' she amended, thinking that one night together hardly amounted to a 'relationship', even if that one night had felt more fulfilling and substantial than any other day of her life. 'It's who he is.'

Alarm darkened Prue's face and Carrie could practically see all the horrifying options flying through her head.

The last thing she wanted to do was worry her mother further, so she took a deep breath. 'The father is Damon Meyer.'

'Damon Meyer? The son of Jacob Meyer?'

'Yes.'

Her mother blew out a stunned breath and Carrie knew she was thinking of the tragic way Jacob had lost his life.

The latest, highly anticipated Meyer-Randolph venture—a gentrification project in a run-down area of Chicago—had not been long underway. Jacob had made it a condition of his inclusion in the project that the existing homes and businesses were safeguarded and incorporated into the new development plans. However, not long after construction had begun, and he'd left to attend to another of his projects in Europe, Sterling Randolph had betrayed that promise in a bid to increase profits. The residents had been forced to leave their properties with little or no notice and with nowhere to go.

Anger at that turn of events had reverberated across the city, sparking enormous protests. When Jacob had learned of the double-cross, it had been too late to undo Sterling's actions, but he'd hastily returned to the city anyway, to try and set things right. When he had attended a meeting with the local community, one furious resident had shot and killed him.

'Well, that definitely does make it more complicated,' Prue said eventually. Seeing Carrie's miserable expression, she tightened the hand curled over hers in silent support. 'Does Damon know who you are?'

'No. And when he finds out I can't see how he will want anything to do with me or the baby.'

Damon left his team celebrating. They had worked tirelessly these past weeks, showing a determination and a focus that had almost rivalled his own. Their pitch to Caldwell had been flawless, so they deserved their night of jubilation.

He, however, would not be celebrating until he had a signed contract in his possession and Randolph's business obituary was being written.

But before he returned to his Mayfair home he stopped off at an exclusive bar for a nightcap.

A lone woman sat at the other end of the bar, and Damon remembered his earlier vow to find a companion to enjoy the night with. But the inviting smile of her deep red lips left him cold, and Damon turned away to savour his drink alone.

She wasn't Carrie. That was the problem.

Because, as much as he didn't want to admit it, there'd been something special about Carrie Miller of Santa Barbara.

Not for the first time a pang of disquiet chimed in him as he considered her. Something that prompted his brow to furrow…as if there was something about her he should have known but wasn't realising…the source of which he had been thus far unable to put his finger on.

But then, out of nowhere, it hit him.

Miller.

Wasn't Miller the maiden name of Sterling Randolph's second wife? The wife with whom he'd had a daughter?

Having committed every aspect of Randolph's life to memory, he scanned the recesses of his mind for her name.

Caroline.

Carrie?

A buzzing sounded in his ears.

No. It was not possible. It had to be a freak coincidence. Both Caroline and Miller were generic names. It was just an unfortunate quirk of fate.

Damon had almost succeeded in convincing himself of that when he recalled Carrie's adamant stance that nothing could or should happen between them and the way she'd tried to leave the chateau.

'It's complicated. You just need to trust me, Damon. It is better for both of us if this begins and ends tonight.'

They were the words she'd spoken that night. They had made no sense at the time, but in this new context there was no misunderstanding them. She had known exactly who he was, and the awful way in which their lives were connected!

The buzzing in his ears grew louder, accompanied by the heated racing and roaring of his blood and a bitter dread pooling in his stomach.

Picking up his phone, he called his executive assistant Isobel, who answered on the first ring. 'I need you to do a background check. The woman I met in Paris—Carrie Miller. Get me everything you can on her,' he instructed, finding it hard to speak with so much visceral feeling coursing through him.

Demonstrating an even greater efficiency than usual, Isobel delivered the report to him the next morning. Looking at the solemnity of her expression as she handed it over, he felt the tiny piece of hope he'd spent the night clinging to that it was all an error evaporate.

'Tell me,' he instructed, unable to bring himself to look and see it in inviolable black and white.

'She was born Caroline Randolph. The only daughter of Sterling Randolph and Prudence Miller. Started to go by Carrie Miller a few years ago. She lives in Santa Barbara... owns a bakery that is turning a pretty decent profit for a company that's less than five years old.'

'And her relationship with her father?'

Because that was what was really mattered.

'It's hard to tell. Her parents divorced when she was nine, her mother relocated to California and retained primary custody. She doesn't court publicity the way her half-brothers do. If she does have a relationship with Randolph, it's a very private one.'

So it was unlikely that she'd been a spy— but not impossible! Perhaps Randolph had dispatched her to find out what Damon was up to...what edge he had with Caldwell or any other deal under negotiation.

'The two of you meeting in Paris could

just be a crazy coincidence,' Isobel voiced, as though reading his thoughts.

'I'm not sure I believe in a coincidence that big,' he muttered, with quelling severity.

He couldn't afford to—not where the Randolphs were concerned.

'What do you want to do?' she asked, after a long silence.

Damon thought quickly, calculating all the different scenarios at play. There was only one course of action to ensure his plans continued unthreatened.

'Nothing. If she was sent to find information, she didn't get anything. And if it was, as you say, just a coincidence, then showing a reaction could tip my hand to Randolph. So I do nothing. Pretend it never happened. Never think of her again. Never see her again. Just make certain you get a guest list for any events I'm scheduled to be at—ensure she and I don't end up in the same place.'

'Of course.' Isobel nodded, getting to her feet and leaving him alone.

Damon rose from his chair, finally giving in to the nauseating agitation burning through his bloodstream. *She was Randolph's daughter.* How could he have been so stupid as not to see it?

His chest see-sawed as he rewound through

their encounter—all the ways she had mesmerised him, coaxed him into letting his guard down. But never again. From now on he didn't want to think about, lay eyes on, or speak to Carrie Miller—or Caroline Randolph...whatever her name was.

Even without her mother telling her so, Carrie knew she couldn't hold off telling Damon about her pregnancy once it had been confirmed by her doctor. Her calls and emails to his company headquarters, however, had gone unanswered, so when she heard that he was scheduled to attend a children's charity ball in Los Angeles she decided to drive up to LA, where his West Coast headquarters were located.

She left at the break of dawn, eager to get the encounter out of the way and to minimise the chance of being spotted. It was miraculous that they had gone without being sighted together in Paris, particularly since so many of Damon's social outings and female companions were noted in some tabloid or other or on a gossip site.

Since returning home Carrie had more than once suffered brief spasms of anxiety as she had belatedly considered exactly what their being seen together might have unleashed, and there was no guarantee she would be so fortunate again—especially not in Los Angeles, where there were more paparazzi in one square foot than anywhere else on the planet.

If she was caught with Damon and presumed to be his new lover—subjected to the gossip and scrutiny his previous lovers had experienced—she knew it wouldn't take long for her real identity to be uncovered. And the revelation that Jacob Meyer's son and Sterling Randolph's daughter were lovers would be salacious enough to guarantee she would find herself at the centre of a new media storm.

The prospect of her life coming under such intrusive scrutiny for a second time, of being watched and followed and whispered about, was too harrowing to bear.

But it was still quiet when she arrived in LA and made the short walk from where she'd parked her car to Damon's offices. She'd viewed pictures of the building online, but the reality was even more impressive. The space was modern and fresh and bright. The striking glass-fronted building gave way to a contemporary interior with cool white and grey flooring and walls. Low-slung white seats and glass tables were clustered in the corners. An angular reception desk held central position in front of a large pond, and a back

wall of windows led onto a lush green court-
yard scattered with rattan tables and chairs
and benches.

The whole building was a testament to Damon's design and architectural skill, and Carrie couldn't help thinking how it was the polar
opposite to her father's more grand and op-
pressive creations.

But as she made her way to the reception
desk she started to feel more jittery than she
had expected, and almost wished she hadn't
declined her mother's offer to accompany her
in favour of facing Damon alone. Because the
sudden tightness swelling in her chest was
enough to make her want to turn around and
speed back to the sanctuary of Santa Barbara.

But she reminded herself that Damon had a
right to know he was going to be a father—a
right to decide his own level of involvement.
It was not her place to make that decision
for him. And Carrie needed to know where
she and her child stood, or she would spend
the coming years wondering, always thinking of him and speculating on what might
have been.

'Can I help you?' the polished receptionist
asked as Carrie reached the desk, her voice
almost echoing in the early-morning quiet.

'Yes,' Carrie said, before her fear of Damon's reaction overpowered her conviction that she needed and wanted to tell him. 'I need to speak to Damon Meyer. I don't have an appointment,' she added, anticipating the question. 'But if you could just let him know that Carrie Miller is here? Tell him I need to talk to him about... Paris.'

'Mr Meyer doesn't take unscheduled meetings.'

The girl delivered the stock line without a beat of hesitation and an almost pitying smile, and immediately Carrie realised she was probably not the first unsolicited female visitor who had attempted to breach the inner sanctum of Damon Meyer.

It was a timely reminder that she was just one amongst the many, and humiliation burned in her cheeks. But she kept her feet planted in the same spot, rooted there by the vow she had made to her unborn child to do everything she possibly could to reach its father, because it was what her child deserved.

'Please,' she heard herself say. 'I'm sure he has a very busy day, but five minutes is all I need. So if there is anything you can do...'

The plea in her eyes must have been immense, because after a minuscule hesitation the girl picked up the telephone and spoke quietly into it before hanging up, the corners of her mouth tipped down.

'I'm sorry. His day is fully booked.'

Carrie felt like a balloon that had been popped. It had taken every ounce of courage she possessed to get to LA and prepare herself to face Damon. To think that it had all been for nothing and she would have to manage the ordeal all over again was exhausting.

'Okay. Thank you for trying.'

'But…' The girl looked around, then leaned closer. 'I shouldn't tell you this, but the elevator from the underground parking garage is undergoing maintenance, so everyone is having to come in the main entrance.' She gestured to the doors Carrie had walked through. 'Even Mr Meyer. He usually arrives within the next five minutes.'

'Thank you,' Carrie breathed, relief flooding through her that her exertions hadn't been for nothing.

She didn't have to wait more than thirty seconds.

She was still walking away from the reception desk when the doors parted and a man swept through them, enough power radiating from his tall, athletic frame to compel anyone in his path to take a hasty step back.

Damon.

He was exactly as he appeared in her thoughts, only better. A million times better. Tall and lean, but strong. His body was encased in a sophisticated dark navy suit, with a white shirt beneath. He wore no tie and his collar was unbuttoned. He carried his sensuality with ease, but it hit Carrie like a lash of lightning, making everything in her go weak.

He saw her straight away, and that burnished gaze of his landed on her. The fluidity of his movement faltered for the smallest second, and Carrie allowed herself a brief spark of hope that he would be happy to see her.

She was on the cusp of opening her mouth to say something, but then she saw the hardening of his expression—like flesh turning to stone. And her heart stuttered as the ice-cold recognition that at least one of her secrets was no longer so secret seeped through her.

He already knew who she was.

Anguish rolled over her in a single violent wave and she took a pleading step towards him. But Damon was already resuming his long stride, issuing words to the woman at his side and clearly planning to breeze straight past her as though she wasn't there…as though she meant nothing.

It was exactly as she had feared—her Randolph blood marked her out at his enemy, worthy of neither his time nor his civility.

It was the reaction she had readied herself to face—or at least she thought she had—but the dismay strangling her heart was a pain greater than she had known to prepare for.

'Damon, please. Wait. I came here to... I need to talk you. It's... It's important.'

He continued his stride, unmoved and unconvinced, reaching the elevator and stabbing the call button. It was on the tip of her tongue to shout out her pregnancy, just to make him listen, knowing that as soon as he stepped into that lift and the doors closed she'd have lost her opportunity, but she had not lost all her sense.

'Please.'

But he ignored her once again, taking a step into the elevator. And then the doors were sliding shut. Spurred by desperation, Carrie rushed forward and thrust her handbag between the doors, forcing them to part again. Damon's eyes moved to her with silent fury, but she stared fearlessly back at him.

'You will want to hear what I came here to tell you.'

Randolphs were liars. *Fact.* And Damon had witnessed first-hand just how convincing a liar Carrie Miller was.

Yet there was something about the weight in her words that prevented him from beckoning Security and having her bodily removed from his building.

What if the something 'important' was something she knew about her father? Something that he was planning? What if he had somehow learned of Damon's chances on the Caldwell project and was concocting a counter attack that would derail his whole revenge plan? Plotting something that would turn the tables on Damon? Something of that magnitude would surely account for Carrie's stricken and pale expression.

Making a snap decision, he turned to address Isobel, issuing instructions through clenched teeth. 'Reschedule my first meeting and make my apologies, please. Miss Miller and I will be in my office. Ensure no one disturbs us.'

Damon gestured for Carrie to step into the elevator. He stared straight ahead as the doors closed, determinedly not looking at her and resenting every moment of shared space and oxygen—especially when her scent infiltrated the air. Her betrayal still burned within his gut, and even if she was in possession of information that might be valuable, she had a nerve, showing up on his territory and demanding an audience.

Clearly she had inherited her father's gall!

But, sour though he felt, Damon knew he could not roll the dice on whether she was being truthful—not with so much at stake.

Forty seconds later they arrived at his top-floor office. Damon secured the door behind them before striding briskly to stand behind his desk.

'You have five minutes. So whatever information you came to here to impart, I suggest you speak quickly,' he instructed, with taciturn impatience.

Carrie stared back at him, her chin raised and her eyes clear. 'I'm pregnant.'

CHAPTER FOUR

'PREGNANT?' DAMON'S HEART, which had momentarily stopped, restarted at a pace that was worryingly similar to a train about to fly off the tracks. Of all the things he had been preparing himself to hear, that hadn't even made the list!

Through a rapidly descending veil of panic he scanned Carrie's face for any sign of the changes pregnancy wrought, but there was nothing—not that their necessarily would be at only a few months along. He knew little about pregnancy, but enough to know that.

'Are you sure?'

'I wouldn't be bothering you if I wasn't,' she replied, with a composure of tone and expression that was in direct contrast to the sound of his heartbeat pounding in his ears.

'But we were safe. I used protection.'

'It happened anyway.'

Her olive-green eyes continued to look unflinchingly back at him, and in spite of the quiet fury he had nursed since learning her identity, and in spite of all that he had felt when he locked eyes on her moments ago downstairs—a blaze of blistering anger and betrayal and hurt—something hot and heavy leapt into life in his stomach. The yearning to lean over and crush her plump mouth beneath his ripped through him, unexpected and intense.

'I'm ten weeks along. A recent blood test and a doctor's appointment confirmed it. I thought you had a right to know that I am pregnant and that I'm having the baby.'

And there it was again—the impact of those words striking him in the centre of his chest, punching pockets of air from his lungs, making his heart stop and start with a distress that threatened to be his undoing.

Gritting his teeth, Damon tried to breathe through it…tried also to steady his thoughts. But there was only a frighteningly familiar sense of the world spinning out of his control. He could feel the closeness of those inky black tentacles, poised to clamp around his wrists and ankles and drag him back into that abyss that had swallowed him as a boy, when he'd lost his father, and then his mother, and his whole world had been in a million pieces around his feet and there had seemed no way to put it back together again.

But he refused to return to that place.

'I know it's a shock…' Carrie said, watching him somewhat cautiously with her large eyes as he propelled himself to his feet.

His agitated stride carried him to the fridge for a bottle of chilled water and he snapped off the top with a frantic twist of his impatient fingers.

'Me showing up and telling you this… I did try to call, but whenever I tried to make contact I was stonewalled.'

She looked at him almost beseechingly, as if wanting forgiveness for… What? Her unexpected announcement? Did she not realise she needed to repent for bigger sins than *shocking* him?

'You were stonewalled at my instruction,' Damon informed her indifferently, his feet moving once again on orders from his restless body, taking him back in the direction of his desk. 'Because I uncovered who your father was and I didn't want there to be any further contact between us. Naturally I didn't expect you'd be reaching out to inform me that our one night together had resulted in pregnancy.'

His chest heaved yet again at that word and

all it implied. But rather than be overwhelmed by it he focused on the facts of it.

Ten weeks along, she had said. He didn't need to do the maths. He knew exactly how long it had been since they'd been together… since he had explored and tasted every inch of her incredible body. Seventy days. *Ten weeks.*

It wasn't inviolable proof, but nonetheless he found that he believed her. She had lied to him about who she was, providing him with ample reason to doubt every word that came out of her mouth, yet for a reason he could not fully comprehend he believed her.

'No. Of course not.' Carrie dropped her gaze to the floor, twisting her fingers together in front of her stomach. 'How did you find out?'

Because I couldn't let you go, he thought as his gaze moved over the delicate features of her face: eyes as large and captivating as an owl's, lips that were full and tempting, and satin-smooth black hair that was a striking contrast to her pale skin.

She was wearing a summery dress, a design with thin straps and a flouncy skirt that brushed against her lightly tanned legs just above her knees, and that flash of toned flesh was mere inches from where he'd nuzzled her with his lips, kissing higher and higher until he had—

With a suppressed curse, Damon broke himself free from the intoxicating memory and pulled his eyes away. But it was too late. He had lingered in it too long to be unaffected, and beneath the heat of recollection blood surged through his veins and a thudding pulse ignited at the base of his groin.

He sighed, perturbed that for a second time she was appealing to him on a sexual level that was forbidden. 'Does it really matter?' he asked.

'I guess not.'

Her slender throat convulsed and the little colour she'd had in her cheeks seemed to fade. Approaching his desk uneasily, she perched on the edge of one of the duo of chairs facing him. It occurred to Damon that, given she was pregnant, he should have invited her to sit immediately. Irked by his uncharacteristic thoughtlessness, he rose from his seat, extracted another bottle of water from the fridge, decanted it into a glass and placed it in front of her.

She murmured her thanks. After a sip she raised her eyes to him. 'I'm sorry that I didn't tell you who I was.'

Surprise at such a forthright apology rendered him momentarily mute. In the two decades since the scandal, Sterling Randolph had never issued any words of regret or contrition for what had unfolded in the wake of his actions. It had been Damon's assumption that his daughter would have the same problem with atoning. But she offered the words readily and sincerely, and they carried more weight than he would have credited, loosening some of the tension straining his arms and easing the red-hot sting of anger swirling in the hollowed pit of his stomach.

'Answer me one question, Carrie—was our meeting in Paris a coincidence?'

He told himself he was asking because it was all that mattered. Because it concerned the plans he had in motion and he needed to know if they were in jeopardy…if Randolph had some notion of what he was up to. But deep down he wanted to know for himself. He wanted—needed—to know if it had been real, if the emotions and yearnings Carrie had provoked in him had been the product of a true and pure connection, or nothing more than a skilful emotional seduction by a manipulator as practised as her father.

'Yes,' she rushed to respond.

But the quick answer failed to satisfy the drumming ache within him and he didn't know why. It was the answer he had needed to hear after all.

'I had no idea you were at that museum gala. I had no idea who you were when we first locked eyes. I just felt a connection. I only knew when you introduced yourself— but everything I was feeling in that moment was so strong, so compelling, that it just got pushed aside.'

The impression of her words made his heart pump harder as she took a breath, her eyes resting gently on him, as though testing his response. He made sure to betray nothing of his conflicting feelings.

'It wasn't until later that night, maybe even the next morning, that it really hit me. I considered not going to the party at the chateau, but the thought of not seeing you again was.... I had a bad experience with a boyfriend. So these last few years I've avoided dating and relationships. But when I met you and felt such an instant connection I didn't want to walk away.' She sucked in a razor-sharp breath. 'I didn't set out to deceive you, Damon. I planned to tell you as soon as I arrived at the chateau. I wanted to tell you. I tried to tell you.'

'You tried?' His thick brows slammed into one another in condemnation of the fact that she had only *tried.* 'You didn't try very hard, did you?'

It should have been the very first thing she'd said to him. She should have made him listen—said it over and over again until he heard her.

'I did try,' she insisted, with a quiet and steady strength, and suddenly he had a flash of forgotten memory.

'There is something I should mention,' she had said, with a tiny flare of anxiety in her eyes.

Only he hadn't let her speak, not wanting to hear anything that would get in the way of what he wanted—her. His heart quickened with the disquieting recollection.

'And what about when you were so desperate to leave and I asked why? Did you try to tell me then? Because all I remember is you saying it was "complicated."'

'I wanted to tell you, Damon.'

For the first time Carrie's composure slipped. Her voice cracked with emotion, a stripe of colour bloomed across the tops of her cheeks, and the hands resting on her knees curled into fists. She pressed herself forward, her breasts swelling against the line of the dress, and the sight had fire licking a path through his stomach.

'I didn't want to keep it from you, but by

that point it already felt too late. We'd connected…you'd opened up to me…and I… I was scared that once I told you Sterling Randolph was my father the only way you would look at me was the way you're looking at me right now.'

The anguish burning in her olive eyes made a knot form in his stomach—because, romantic dreamer that she was, she had imagined something that could never be. She'd craved something it was impossible for him to give and she would never truly be able to understand why. Because the truth of that day was something that very few people knew.

'You are the daughter of the man who got my father murdered,' he intoned huskily. 'You're *Caroline Randolph*. How am I meant to look at you?'

'I am not Caroline Randolph,' she asserted, in a tone that was far more venomous than anything he'd previously heard her use.

It made him wonder. Wonder why she lived her life under her mother's name. Wonder why she fought so hard against the name of her birth—a name that signalled privilege and wealth among other things. Wonder if that reason, like so many bad things did, originated with her father.

'The only person who calls me Caroline is

my father. To everyone else I'm just Carrie. Carrie Miller. And with regard to my father, and being a Randolph—'

Damon held up his hand, cutting off her protest. Silencing his own curiosity. 'It doesn't matter. Whatever you call yourself, you're still Sterling Randolph's daughter.'

The daughter of the monster who had caused his father's death. Hungering for her didn't change that. Nothing could change that, however much he was wishing differently in this strange moment. And it was in that moment that Damon recognised that whilst it was the lie that had spurred his initial anger, it was not what had sustained it. It was what the lie had been about. She was a Randolph. That precluded anything from ever happening between them again, and his feelings on that were not quite so clear-cut.

'His actions put my father in a grave, Carrie. It's just that simple.'

She fought the emotion that was changing her expression. 'So that's it? What happened between us in Paris goes to the top of your list of regrets?'

Damon started to shake his head, but then stopped. He would never regret that night, but admitting it aloud would accomplish nothing. It *had* to be consigned to the past. Didn't it?

It felt as if his future hinged on this moment—this answer. He would either continue traversing the path he had started down long ago, storming towards his revenge, or lean into this sudden bend, leading goodness knew where. Back to all that she had made him want in Paris? But that, too, would inevitably end in loss and pain. *More* pain.

Clearly interpreting his contemplative silence as his answer, Carrie folded her arms across her chest. 'And the child we made together? Do you have any interest in knowing it?'

'It is not that simple,' he stated through his tightly clenched jaw, avoiding looking too closely at the dark emotion flaring in the green depths of her gaze. 'For the reasons we've just gone through, our circumstances are…complex.'

'I'll take that as a no.'

She was angry. The look on her face told him that. But she was also not surprised. She'd known his answer before he'd even issued it, just as she had known how he would look at her upon learning her given name, and her expected disappointment settled on him like a ton of bricks.

But what was the alternative option? They

raised the child together, a Randolph and a Meyer? That was ludicrous.

'I will have an account set up in your name,' he said, surprised by the hoarseness of his own voice. 'Neither of you will want for anything.'

Carrie pushed herself to her feet. 'There's no need for you to do that. I'm perfectly capable of providing for us. I didn't come here to obligate you. I just wanted you to know.'

'There's every reason to do it,' he countered, standing too. 'We made this child together. I have a responsibility.'

Even as he uttered the words he recognised their laughable hypocrisy, and by the sudden flare of colour in her eyes, Carrie did also.

'Obviously I will require a DNA test at some point, to confirm paternity. But I'm aware there are sometimes safety issues involved with such tests, so that can wait until a point at which it doesn't pose a risk to you or...' His eyes dropped to her stomach and he was beset by the sudden desire to touch where his child grew, to splay his hand over her in some kind of paternal pride or possessiveness. 'Or the baby.'

'Fine. But whenever the test happens you should be prepared for a positive result.

You're the only man I've been with in a long time.'

She'd said as much the night they'd made love, but to hear it again pierced him afresh. It had felt like a proprietorial caveman stamp on her, as if he had claimed her, taken her, made her his. That out of all the men on the planet she could have selected from she had wanted him.

When he tried to speak again, his throat was thick. 'Whatever you need in terms of doctors or accommodation, get in touch.' He offered her a piece of paper. 'This email address and phone number connects you directly to my executive assistant, Isobel. She will take care of anything you require.'

Carrie examined the scribble with a frighteningly blank expression. 'Well, I came here to tell you I was pregnant, and I've done that, so I'll let you get back to your day. Goodbye, Damon.'

She didn't wait for him to return the pleasantry. She turned and with her head held high strode from his office, leaving her scent in the air, an unsettled feeling scratching at the skin of his chest and a sudden rushing impulse to run after her.

Carrie jabbed at the button to call for the elevator, fighting the burning tears that were attacking the backs of her eyes. She did not want to cry. She wanted to be strong for herself, and for the child she carried, but every inch of her was wounded and aching with a disappointment she had little reason to feel so acutely. Not when the meeting had played out exactly as she had feared it would.

Damon had been angry that she'd lied. Shocked that she was pregnant. Reviled by her DNA and unwilling to be an active parent to a baby with Randolph blood.

He had every right to be furious with her, but the way he had turned his feelings off so completely had left her cold with shock. She'd believed they had shared more than that. But the man she had faced today had been cool and unyielding. Emotionally unreachable. It brought ugly, unbidden memories to the centre of her mind…memories of other emotionally unavailable men, hard and selfish men, on whom she had wasted too many tears.

Her father, for one.

How many times has she stood in front of him, desperately trying to reach him, to make a connection, only to be regarded by a blank stare? And that awful day when Nate's true intentions had become clear. She'd needed his support and his comfort but had been met only with his cold recrimination. She'd been crying, humiliated, her heart crushed, and he hadn't even hugged her.

Her fingers curled into a fist, closing around the card Damon had given her with the contact information written on—contact information for his PA, not even for him!

Her upset coalesced and hardened into an anger that throbbed in every inch of her body. She wasn't afraid of raising her child alone. Her mother had pretty much raised Carrie single-handedly, and she was a glowing example of what was possible. With the promised support of her mother and her grandparents, who were twin pillars in her life, she was in no doubt that she would successfully and happily raise her child in a secure and loving environment.

And yet Carrie was aware of the open wound left by not having a relationship with one's father. She would prefer it if the same fate wasn't inflicted on her child.

But Damon was making a decision that was all about him. He hadn't given a single second's consideration to the child they had made together and what was best for him or her. He was too consumed by the past to give any thought to the future, stuck in his uncompromisingly rigid position.

Just like her father, who had only ever seen

the world though his own eyes, his own ambitions and greed. He had never donated a moment's consideration to anyone else—not his sons, nor his wife or his daughter.

With a ping, the elevator announced its arrival and the doors slid open, but Carrie's feet wouldn't move. She had always been cowed by her father's unyieldingness, never arguing with him. Because he was shockingly incapable of seeing another perspective from his entrenched position and because his favour was earned through silence. And more than anything she had longed for his favour. His love.

She had felt the same powerlessness in Damon's office, faced with his animosity, and had retreated to her default position of silence and acquiescence, hoping that if she didn't aggravate the situation further it would work out the way she hoped. But staying silent had only ever left her hurt and resentful. It hadn't enabled any relationship with her father.

Carrie didn't want to repeat that pattern with another person, and she didn't want to make the same mistakes—especially not when her child would be adversely affected. It was past time she learned to use her voice, to advocate for what she wanted and needed and what was best for her child.

Turning on her heel, she marched back into his office.

Damon spun with a startled look as the door crashed against the wall. 'Carrie, what—?'

'No! You had your turn to speak and I listened. So now you're going to listen to me.'

She drew in a fortifying breath, her courage wobbling as she felt the full force of his authoritative persona directed her way. He was clearly unused to being addressed so forcefully.

'I'm not under any illusions about my father. What he did to your father was awful, and you have every right to hate him. But that has nothing to do with this baby,' she said, her hands moving across her still-flat stomach. 'And it shouldn't have any influence on how you feel about this pregnancy.'

Pausing to draw a much-needed breath, she tried not to be diverted by the sheer magnificence of him, still and tall and straight-backed, polished eyes fixed on her. Their connection had been forged at first sight, and she felt its reigning power every time their gazes collided, making her shake and shiver all the way down to her toes.

'If you don't want to be involved, that's fine. I have no problem doing this on my own. But if the only reason you don't want to be involved is because one quarter of this child's DNA comes from Sterling Randolph, then you're acting like a fool and doing the child a huge disservice. Because you got one thing right—you *do* have a responsibility. To be there. To love it. To help it become the greatest and happiest person it can be, living a life that makes it happy. You grew up without your father, Damon. You know what that feels like. The emptiness, the sorrow... And you blame my father for taking yours away from you. Do you really want to let him be the reason you don't know your child too?'

The dark silence of his house greeted Damon when he arrived home from the charity ball. He tapped the control panel on the wall to bring up the lights before freeing himself from the tuxedo jacket, pulling apart the bowtie and ripping open the top buttons of his shirt.

Finally, he could draw a breath.

The children's ball was an important evening to him. It was the one event he attended without fail every year, often working his schedule around the date.

Damon had learned the importance of giving back from his father. When he'd lived, Jacob Meyer had been an actively involved patron of a particular charity that focused its efforts and resources on children in difficult situations. It had seemed only natural that Damon continued his efforts and, truth be told, Damon felt a great affinity for lost and struggling children. Having been robbed of his father, and then abandoned by his mother, he was aware of those struggles and the emotions that could be overpowering.

Anything he could do to ease those difficulties Damon was willing to do—including showing his face at the heavily attended ball to raise the charity's profile and boost the generosity of the donations given. As much as he sometimes loathed the inane small talk and huge egos, he was more than happy to help. But that night the function had seemed interminable, and from the moment he had arrived all he had been focused on was when he could leave.

Pouring himself a glass of smooth Cabernet, he walked out to the large terrace off the master bedroom of his house high up in the Bird Streets. As the name suggested, it was perched up in the Hollywood Hills, with the lights of Los Angeles glittering in the near distance. It was usually one of the few places he was able to find a rare moment of tranquillity and perspective, with his father's most famous construction standing proudly amongst all the other towers of downtown LA, its top light like a beacon just for Damon, but there was no peace to be found tonight.

Only noise.

Fatherhood had never been an ambition of his. Nor a consideration. He was too focused on bringing down Sterling Randolph to give any thought to the concerns of normal people, like marriage and children. No man could serve two masters, after all, and Damon had long known that his purpose in life was a pursuit that required *all* of him. And, whilst he had made himself enormously successful along the way, Damon would not consider his life a success until he had settled that score and avenged his father.

That was the purpose behind everything he did.

That was the cause to which he had dedicated his life.

And there was no place for a family amongst that.

Except now he had no choice about that. There was going to be a child. There already was a child, growing in the womb of the daughter of his enemy. A child with Randolph blood.

Damon took a long sip of his wine, his temples feeling tight.

He didn't have anything to offer—at least not emotionally. His heart had turned to stone after his father's death and had remained in his chest as a useless rock. And yet his decision to be uninvolved, other than financially, was not resting easily within him. He had not rested easily since the moment he'd made it.

A child deserved more than a big house and a healthy back account. It needed the security of unfailing, unconditional love and two present, interested parents. Every day of his life his father had demonstrated that to him. Jacob Meyer had always shown Damon how much he loved him, how important his happiness was to him.

Did he not owe his own flesh and blood the same devotion? Anything less than that would be unconscionable—especially when he knew the cost of parental rejection. How the child was always the one to pay the ultimate price in an inability to open up and trust and love. In the fear of doing so.

When he had needed her the most, his mother had turned away from him and left him behind. He hadn't been forced to contend with poverty or homelessness, so he had been luckier than many—and he never allowed himself to forget that—but it had still hurt and confused him. Would he really doom his own child to the same lifetime of confusion and questioning what they had done wrong, why they hadn't been enough for their parent to stay?

No, he could not pass on that pain. He would not author a legacy of heartache and mistrust.

Had he been thinking clearly earlier that day, he would have known there was no way he could be separate from his child. It was unthinkable. But he had not been thinking clearly. The decision he'd reached had been birthed by panic and fear. And not because Carrie was a Randolph but because when Carrie, in all her loveliness, had stood before him, everything she'd made him feel and think had been threatening.

Threatening to draw down his barriers and throw him off course.

Threatening the life he had built and shaking its very foundations.

And he had reacted defensively.

Blinded by panic, he had thought only of ending the discomfort, of making himself safe again, and he was ashamed of how selfish he had been in those moments, considering only himself and not the wellbeing of his child.

He certainly hadn't needed Carrie to march back into his office and tell him about the mistake he was making. On some level he had already known it. But her speech had crystallised it for him far sooner than he would have done it on his own.

To burden his son or daughter with the sins of its grandfather was wrong. And to miss out on the opportunity to know his child and be a steady and supportive presence, just as his own father had been, would be an enormous mistake.

But nothing else would change.

Carrie might not be his enemy, but she was still forbidden fruit. The only relationship he would have with her was one that was necessary for their child to be raised with both its parents.

And as for Sterling Randolph…

He still needed to pay for what he had done and Damon would ensure he did—and soon. The moment the ink of his signature was dry on the Caldwell contract was the moment when Sterling Randolph's world would collapse faster than a house of cards.

CHAPTER FIVE

CARRIE EXTRACTED THE tray of muffins from the oven and set it on the cooling rack, smiling at the sounds of delight from her young students. These informal baking lessons with a small group of adolescents from a local children's home had come about organically, largely because of Carrie's friendship with the woman who ran the home. She always felt as if she was doing something good in those lessons, paying something forward, and it was for that reason she had ignored the pit in her stomach the size of the Grand Canyon and forced herself up and out of bed that morning, refusing to be pressed into a wallowing misery.

Carrie had too many good things in her life to let Damon's rejection define her. And she would forge ahead with that life—a life that made her happy because it was what defined her. Her creativity. Her hard work. The community that supported her and which she gave back to. *Not* her name. And if Damon couldn't recognise that…well, *screw him*.

Carrie had wanted to believe that the connection they'd shared was strong enough to override the negativity of her name, but that had been just another wish from her hopeful, foolish heart.

Like many others who'd passed through her life Damon, the moment he had discovered her name, had thought it was all that mattered. But unlike all those others who had wanted to use her because of it, regarding her as some kind of chip with which they could bargain their way into a better life, Damon viewed it as a plague that needed to be avoided.

As much as she wished it was different, she would not bruise her knees praying for him to change his mind and show up on her doorstep. She refused to wait and hope, even though she was feeling the pinch of every silent hour and day that went by the way she had with her father when she'd been a young girl. She had waited and waited for him, hoping with every breath and every beat of her heart that he would show up and show her how much he cared—only to end up crying disappointed tears into her mother's shoulder.

There would be no more tears. She'd cried too many over men already. Her father. Nate. And now Damon. She was done with giving other people the power to hurt her.

And after yesterday she wasn't sure she wanted to see Damon ever again anyway. What she had seen of him made her think that she and her baby might be better off without him in their lives.

'Carrie?' Marina, the bakery's manager, popped her head around the door separating the café from the kitchen. 'Are you almost done in here? There's someone at the counter asking for you.'

Carrie frowned to herself as she helped the kids to box up the muffins she'd taught them to make. 'I don't have any appointments scheduled for this afternoon.'

She had deliberately been keeping her afternoons light, knowing that was when her pregnancy sickness and fatigue began to take their toll.

'I don't think it's about a cake order. I think this is a *personal* visit.'

Her busy hands stilled, her spine beginning to tingle at her friend's choice of tone. 'Who is it?'

'He didn't offer a name. But tall, dark-haired, a little Latin-flavoured and heart-stoppingly handsome about sums him up.'

Damon.

Her heart thumped so hard that her chest momentarily hurt. Some crazy part of her was joyous at the prospect of laying eyes on him, even as she recoiled at the thought of facing him again.

But surely it couldn't be him? He'd made his feelings painfully clear in his office, and when he hadn't been roused enough by her impassioned plea to chase her down before she reached the exit of his building she had understood the chance of him changing his mind wasn't just slim, it was non-existent. So it seemed highly unlikely that he had taken time out of his day to make the journey to Santa Barbara and was actually standing in her place of business.

Yet…who else could it be?

Heart hammering, Carrie took the few steps over to the doorway for visual confirmation, fully expecting it to be someone else. However, when she pressed open the door just enough to peep through she gasped as her eyes immediately locked on Damon. He was standing side on to her, so she could only see him in profile, but there was no mistaking him. No mistaking that proud and indomitable stance. Or the way her pulse fluttered and flipped in recognition of it.

In an immaculately tailored grey suit and a pale blue shirt that greatly enhanced the golden hue of his skin and the bitter darkness of his hair he looked frustratingly, mouth-wateringly good. Her heart caught as, even from afar, the impact of him pierced her sharp and deep, making her weak for him all over again, making her skin tingle with hunger to feel his touch. And she cursed herself for it. After yesterday, how was it still possible that her blood was singing at the sight of him?

Quickly Carrie released the door, taking a hasty step back from it as the tingles deepened to full-body tremors and her mind whirred. What was he doing here? Hadn't he already said everything he needed to say? Hadn't he inflicted enough damage upon her heart?

So what on earth…?

Unless…

Her frazzled mind could drum up only one reason for his unexpected appearance. But… surely not? Surely after everything he'd said yesterday Damon hadn't actually changed his mind about being a father to their child…?

Damon couldn't quite believe it. Not only had he voluntarily entered a business owned by a

Randolph, but he also didn't loathe it on first sight. The space, simply named The Bakehouse, was actually rather inviting. The pale walls, wooden tables and chairs and modern, warm lighting all combined to create a welcoming and comfortable interior that relaxed its occupants without their awareness, making them want to sit and while away a few easy hours.

Casting his assessing gaze around as he was made to wait, he recognised Carrie's bright energy everywhere.

The gaggle of voices behind him had Damon turning sharply and eyeing the group of pre-teen youngsters emerging from what he suspected was the kitchen. Carrie was bringing up the rear, and as his eyes caught on her they stuck. She wore ripped jeans and a simple tee that highlighted her narrow waist, her slim legs and the generous curve of her breasts, which definitely had a new and welcome fullness, and the sight of her had him struggling against the instinct to reach out, pull her against his hard body and plunder her mouth until she was boneless and begging beneath him.

Seeing himself doing exactly that had him throbbing with agonising anticipation, even whilst simultaneously fighting a savage burst of annoyance. She was off-limits, and he couldn't comprehend why his brain was having so much trouble computing that message or why his body was failing to respond with obedience.

Burying his hand deep in the pockets of his trousers, where they would be prevented from reaching out and grabbing her on the orders of a wayward neuron, he watched with mounting impatience as she exchanged a few smiling words with the woman who was clearly the youngsters' chaperone before seeing them out through the door and waving them off with a promise for 'next time.'

Slowly, she turned and met his waiting gaze, folding her arms across her chest as she did so. 'You were looking for me?' she asked, her clear olive eyes and smooth expression offering no hint as to whether she was happy to see him or not.

He found that neutrality disconcerting. Not that he knew why. He was not there for her, but for their child, he reminded himself.

'Yes. I wanted to speak with you.' He glanced at their surroundings with a small frown, at the patrons too close for comfort. 'Is there somewhere private we could talk?'

Carrie led him to a small office. It was

a bright and happy space, but she remained maddeningly neutral.

'Why are you here, Damon? Because it seems to me you said everything you needed to say yesterday.'

Her bluntness caught him off guard. 'I said a lot yesterday, I know. And I'm here because I think I was too hasty. As you said, the news was a shock, and I spoke under the pressure of too many emotions,' he admitted on a slight growl, as with rising agitation he could feel them stirring once more.

What was it about this woman that could make him feel so much in such a short span of time? He drew in a breath, but it was like attempting to steady a ship being buffeted by the violent waves of an approaching storm.

'The truth is there's no way I could live happily not knowing my child. It would be impossible.'

'So you're saying you've changed your mind?' Carrie surmised, with an enquiring arch of her eyebrow that managed to convey the depth of her disbelief.

Damon knew it was no less than he deserved.

'You *do* want to be involved?'

'Yes. I'm going to be involved,' he asserted, holding her gaze and refusing to release it even as a treacherous heat stirred at the base of his stomach.

'Okay,' she said finally. 'Good.'

Damon didn't look too closely at the way her approval made him feel pounds lighter. 'Anyway, that's why I'm here. I thought we should talk again. Start the conversation over. Begin afresh.'

'Yes. We should do that…' With a nervous dip of her throat, she looked at her watch. 'Erm… I don't close up here for another few hours. But you can stay and have some coffee and cake—or I can meet you after?'

'Do you have plans for dinner?' Damon queried, the question catching him as unawares as it clearly did her. Because dinner had certainly not been part of his plan when he had decided to seek Carrie out in Santa Barbara.

But he did not want to conduct their conversation when she was working and they could be overheard or interrupted at any moment. It would be close to dinner time by the time she finished work, he argued inside his head, and, Carrie being pregnant, it was important she ate a decent meal. It had nothing to do with the way she was standing across from him, with her wide glowing eyes blinking up at him, making him long for a further

opportunity to be near to her, to have the freedom to fix his gaze on her and watch her until
his eyes were dry.

'No, I don't,' she responded, shaking her
head tentatively.

'You do now.'

CHAPTER SIX

CARRIE WAS NERVOUS as she arrived at the hotel where she'd agreed to meet Damon for dinner. He'd messaged her a short while earlier, saying he'd booked one of the resort's luxurious private bungalows and arranged for dinner to be provided there, so she'd set off along the winding pathways through the colourful jungle gardens the resort was famous for. But with every step she took her pulse beat harder—too hard—in her veins.

She knew she should be happy that Damon had changed his mind, but all Carrie felt was troubled. Because how could she be sure he meant it? A day ago he'd declared the complexities of their situation insurmountable, so what had changed so quickly? And what was to stop him from changing his mind again tomorrow? Or in a year?

Carrie wanted to believe he was sincere, because she wanted her child to grow up with two loving parents, but she remembered all the other times in her life when men had spoken words with no real intent or emotion behind them. All the other times she'd trusted and been let down.

And it was not only her own heart she was responsible for now, but her child's—she had to proceed with caution if she was to prevent history from repeating itself.

Drawing in a steadying breath, she knocked at the door of the bungalow. Damon answered it within seconds, flashing her a perfunctory smile and beckoning her in. His shirtsleeves were rolled up and several top buttons open, exposing his strong, hair-dusted forearms and a triangle of smooth gold chest, and that flash of skin had Carrie's throat drying even more as she remembered the hot smoothness of his body, the feel of him beneath her tongue.

For the briefest of moments everything else she was feeling rolled away, leaving only that delicious, stomach-tightening hum of attraction.

But it was only a moment.

Because she couldn't just forget the side of him she had seen yesterday. A side that was cold and rigid and selfish. All the things her father was.

'Can I get you something to drink?' he offered pleasantly, leading her along a corridor and into the body of the bungalow, then out through French doors to a red-tiled patio, where a table was already set for dinner with fine white china, crystal glasses and a vase of fresh-cut, short-stemmed pink and white roses.

'Water is fine, thank you.'

'The servers should be back shortly with the food. I hope it's not a problem, us eating here instead of a restaurant? But I thought this way we'd have more privacy.'

'No, it's fine. And you're right about the privacy factor. The restaurants are always booked to capacity.'

It was one less thing for her to worry about, at least—that they would be overheard and her secret exposed. At some point she knew there would be publicity—Damon's public status would ensure that—but it was something she was doing her best not to think about.

'You're familiar with the resort, then?' he asked, returning with their drinks.

The graze of their fingers as he handed her a glass of water detonated sparks all over her skin, making her hot and tingly everywhere. She took a healthy gulp, seeking to put out those small fires igniting in too many corners of her body.

'I make the cakes for a fair few of the weddings that get held here, so I'm here often enough.'

'You've clearly built a thriving business,' Damon complimented her. 'I thought your bakery was an impressive space.'

'Thank you.'

Carrie knew what he was doing with his easy smiles and courteous conversation. He was trying to charm her into forgetting all about the previous day. But it wasn't going to work. She wouldn't fall for charm again— not after Nate—not even if being the focus of Damon's clever mind and rich gaze was making her heart race. Making her remember all the reasons she'd wanted to go to bed with him in the first place.

Selecting a roll from the bread basket in the centre of the table, she began to spread a light layer of butter on it, needing to focus on something other than him and the heat sweeping across her skin as he continued to watch her.

'I can't help but be curious about that group of adolescents you had there when I arrived,' he said, startling her with the unexpected query.

'The kids? They're from a children's home down the coast. I host baking lessons for them every few weeks.' She took another cooling sip of water. 'Why do you ask?'

'Just curious.' Damon stared at her, long and hard, as if she was a knot he couldn't untangle. 'It's nice of you to do that.'

And because she was Sterling Randolph's daughter he thought she'd be incapable of doing something nice?

'It's not that big a deal. I just show them the basics. I started it just to give them a few hours of fun, but some have really taken to baking. I actually ended up hiring one of the older girls for a few hours on weekends.'

'I'm sure that to those kids, in the situation they're in, it is a big deal. To have someone give them that time and attention, to show an interest in them and be willing to invest in them…it will mean a lot.'

Carrie tilted her head, now curious herself. 'You say that like you have some experience of their situation?'

He lifted his shoulders in a nonchalant shrug. 'An organisation I support focuses its efforts on young people in tough circumstances. Most of them, for various reasons, are alone in the world. A lot of what we try to do with is show them that the future doesn't have to be hopeless, find them opportunities similar to what you're offering. Something to give them practical skills or experience… something to interest or excite them.'

'You said "we,"' Carrie blurted, thinking aloud. '"A lot of what *we* try to do." You're involved personally with those kids?'

Damon nodded slowly. 'I guess you'd call it big-brothering, or mentoring. Basically, I'm just someone to be there for them, to talk to them, give advice, offer support and ideas. You look surprised,' he commented, his eyes raking over the expression she'd failed to keep neutral.

'In my experience men of your status and success would much prefer to write a cheque with an extra zero on it than give anything of themselves.'

'I can't say that surprises me,' he bit back, streaks of hot colour flaring in his eyes like a warning shot, because he knew exactly who she was referring to and did not like the comparison. 'But I think you'll find I bear very little resemblance to the men you've experienced in your life.'

Carrie had to clamp down on her tongue to keep from firing back that he'd resembled her father pretty spectacularly yesterday. Because it would only antagonise him. And she wasn't there to fight, but to find some clarity. Either to confirm or dismiss her concern that he was woven from the same cloth as her father.

And learning that he didn't just support charities financially but actually participated in their work made him as different from her father as it was possible to be. More than that, he cared about those kids he mentored—Carrie had heard it in his voice. And didn't that say something about the type of man he was? The kind of father he would be?

It was certainly encouraging, but she needed more solid proof than that. She needed to know without a shadow of a doubt that she could rely on him and his word. That their child would be able to rely on him in a way she had never been able to depend on Sterling Randolph. And that was exactly what she was trying to discern as she matched his unflinching regard—almost as if, if she looked hard enough, she'd be able to see through to his heart.

A knock at the door signalling the arrival of their food pierced the terse silence, and without a word Damon rose to let the servers in. A few moments later they were gone again, and a feast of steaming dishes was spread across the table.

'How have you been feeling?' Damon

asked as they began to eat. 'With the pregnancy? I should have asked that sooner. I apologise for not doing so.'

Touched by the apology, and the query after her wellbeing, she felt the stiff line of her spine soften.

'Not too bad. A little more tired than usual, and the morning sickness is disruptive. I'm not sure why it's called morning sickness when it lasts all day, but I'm getting through it.'

'You're okay to be working?'

'Of course. Besides, it's *my* business. I need to be there to run it.'

'Being on your feet all day is not a problem?'

'Not at this stage of pregnancy, no.'

'I only ask as you said you're more tired than normal.'

'The doctor said that's fairly typical, so I don't think being at work is the culprit. Obviously it may get more problematic as the pregnancy progresses.' She paused. 'I actually have my first ultrasound appointment tomorrow. If you're still around, you might like to come.'

'I'd like that,' he replied definitively. 'I'll be there.'

'Good.'

Carrie had half expected him to fob her off, the way her father always did, and she felt a small bubble of joy that he hadn't. That he was ready and willing to back up his declaration with action.

And suddenly she could not put off asking one of her pressing questions any longer. 'Damon, what changed your mind about… all of this?'

He spent a moment considering, lashes drawn down over his cocoa-rich gaze. Then, 'As I said earlier, it was a shock that I didn't react well to. I spoke in haste.'

From the way his brows drew together in a tight pinch, Carrie knew he really was unhappy with himself over his initial reaction.

'And you were right in what you said,' he went on. 'I lost the opportunity to have a relationship with my father because of yours. But there is no need for our child to suffer in the same way, for the past to claim another victim.'

The delicious morsel of food in her mouth turned to ash and Carrie had to force it down her throat. So it was about her father. Yet again.

The ease she had been starting to feel evaporated. Carefully, she set down her fork. 'I don't really know how ask this in a neat way, so I'll just ask it. In LA, you said you couldn't be involved because my being my father's daughter made it too complex. Well, this child is his grandchild. Are you able to separate those things? Are you going to be able to love this child?'

When Damon raised his eyes in response to her question and met her waiting gaze, the tension between them ballooned so thick that it would have needed a chainsaw to cut through it.

'It's my child. Of course I will love it.'

The look he dealt her could have sliced her in half.

'You doubt that?' he asked.

'I don't want to,' she answered earnestly. 'But you feel such animosity for my father... I don't want this child to be raised amongst bitterness and enmity. I only want it to know a happy life.'

'That's all I want too.'

Carrie looked away. There was so much nervousness jangling within her that she needed a second to compose herself. How could she frame her fears in the right way? How could she explain that she wanted to believe him but was terrified of how alive the past was in his present—a present that was complicated enough without being made murkier by ancient shadows?

'Are you really going to be able to deal with having a child with Randolph blood? Can you look beyond that? Because if you think you can't, or that at some point you may want to walk away, you should bow out now. I told you yesterday, I can do this alone. And having no father at all is better than having one who's uninterested, or hateful—or, worse, one who checks out.'

Damon's expression had hardened as she spoke.

'That's not going to happen. And I will not let you conjure these scenarios as a pretext to exclude me from my child's life,'

'I don't want to exclude you. I am the person who braved coming to see you so you would know about the baby. All I'm asking is if you're one hundred percent sure of your decision. Because if you're not...' she had to take a breath, draw on all her courage to speak the following words '... I have reservations about you being involved.'

For the longest moment he stared back at her without moving, without even blinking. Then, 'Let's be clear. I *am* going to be involved. We can sort it out amicably, between us, or we can involve lawyers. But my involvement is not in question.'

Carrie felt her whole body react with a spasm of fear to the threat of litigation, and knew she must have paled, because a second later Damon speared his fingers through his hair and exhaled a heavy breath.

'I'm sorry. I didn't mean that to come out as a threat.'

'It certainly sounded like one.'

'The truth is, this is not a situation I ever expected to find myself in. Dealing with an unplanned pregnancy… Never mind being in it with—' He managed to stop his words, but a line of guilty colour streaked through his gaze before he could avert it, and it was that look that said everything he didn't want to say.

'Go on—say it,' Carrie urged, already knowing that he was thinking it each time he looked at her. That it was *all* he thought about. He'd changed his mind about the baby, but not about her. 'You didn't imagine being in this scenario with the daughter of the man you hate. The daughter of the man you hold responsible for killing your father.'

His gaze turned to granite. 'He *did* kill my father.'

'He didn't pull the trigger.'

This time it was anger that flashed in his eyes. Cold and lethal. 'So you're defending him now?'

'No.' She sighed, feeling the heavy weight of the past pressing against her chest and causing her anxiety to surge. 'I'm not. But don't you see you're proving my point? This should only be about the baby—about what is best for him or her. Not my father and what he is, what he's done. He has *zero* involvement in this.'

'He's your father, Carrie,' Damon scoffed.

'Yes, he is. Which, by the way, is something I have no control over. And, like I tried to tell you the other day, he and I barely have a relationship.'

Leaning back in his seat, Damon looked as if he was processing the information, but Carrie was not fooled into thinking that he was relaxed. She could see by the set of his body that he was still primed to pounce.

'So he won't be in the baby's life?'

'I won't prevent him from meeting his grandchild, if that's what you're asking. He's my father, and my door is always open to him. But as far as him being involved—that's unlikely.'

It was a painful truth, not made any less

painful by the long years Carrie had had to come to terms with his indifference.

'Unless something is directly about him or his business, my father has very little interest in it. As this baby is about neither, I can't imagine him being any more a feature in its life than he was in mine. He doesn't even know I'm pregnant,' she shared, with a shrug to disguise the constant hurt she felt over the state of their relationship.

'He doesn't?'

'No.'

By the way Damon's eyebrows flew up with a surprise he could not contain, Carrie knew it meant that he was *finally* listening and hearing. And once he understood that her connection to her father was in a large part in name only, maybe his attitude to her would soften and they could start contemplating how to navigate the future, rather than arguing over the past.

'As I said, we don't have a close relationship.'

'Have you told anyone? About the baby?'

'My mother, of course. And my grandparents. They were surprised, but they're excited. They've all offered their help.'

'So you're planning on raising the baby here? In Santa Barbara?'

'Yes. This is my home. It's where my family is…my work is. It's where I'm happy.'

Damon nodded as though he had anticipated that. 'At present, I'm based primarily on the East Coast. But, as you no doubt know, I have offices in several cities—including Los Angeles. I also have a house there. Now, I have no problem making the West Coast my primary base, but I'm not sure my living full-time in LA is the most suitable arrangement,' he disclosed with a pragmatic tilt of his dark head. 'I think it would be far better for me to find a home here, near to you. Obviously I would need to commute to my LA office daily, and I'll need to travel for business. But so did my father, and he always made it work. As long as our child has a stable place to call home…'

Carrie held up her hand. Her head was spinning so fast she was liable to fall over, even though she was sitting. 'Wait—I'm sorry. You'll buy a house *here*? In Santa Barbara?'

'Yes. That way it will be easy for us to co-parent. The child can go between us without having any if its fundamentals change. Same nanny, same school, same friends…you get the idea. That way we'll be able to have a flexible arrangement that suits us both.'

Her mouth had gone bone-dry. He wanted

to move to Santa Barbara? To co-parent? It was the last thing she had expected. She wasn't sure what arrangement she had been expecting, but it definitely wasn't this. Quickly, Carrie considered the implications of it—Damon being in her life, day in and day out—and her heart quickened, something she couldn't name thudding beneath her breast.

'So when you said you wanted to be involved, you meant...'

'That I want to be a full-time parent to my child, yes,' Damon clarified, eying her without concern. 'I have no desire to be a part-time father, Carrie. I want to be with my child on a daily basis. I want a relationship from the start. My father was a hugely important figure in my life. I always knew he loved me and was there for me, whatever else he had going on. If I'm anything less than that to my own child, I'll have failed.'

His passionate intensity left her speechless, and she could only stare into his handsome face, transfixed by the determination blazing there. Determination to be a good father, a good man. And in that instant Carrie trusted entirely in his promise to be present for their child. He was willing to change his life for it. To prioritise it.

It was a love she'd never known from her

own father, and that made emotion stick at the back of her throat. Because for the first time she actually felt that it all might work out. That she and Damon would be able to make it work because they had common ground in wanting the best for their child.

'And since there is no possibility of you and I being together romantically, this seems like the best available alternative scenario.'

She went cold all over. Her heart clenched and her eyes burned. The sting of his words pierced so deep that for a moment she forgot to breathe.

'Right. Of course. It's the next best thing,' she agreed, hoping he hadn't noticed the beat of stunned silence before she spoke.

Then, picking up her fork, she moved it around her plate, keeping her hands busy and her eyes lowered.

'You're crying,' Damon stated, his eyes burning a hole in her.

'No. I'm not,' Carrie insisted, even as she kept her eyes downwards. It was bad enough that she was upset, but that he could *see* it…

'Yes. You are.'

Reaching out his hand, he extended two fingers under her chin and tilted her face up, baring to his gaze the sparkling moisture that sat on her lashes and blurred her vision.

Beneath her skin sensation pulsed where his fingers rested. It crackled through her, causing her pulse to leap, her blood to race, her skin to colour. But before the feelings could deepen, and she was forced to remember exactly how good it had felt to be touched and held by him, and before that hunger for him wrote itself across her face, she pulled herself free of his touch.

'Fine.' She braced herself to be honest. 'You said that you never planned on being in this situation. Well, neither did I,' she shared, her voice sounding as brittle as she felt. 'When I pictured having a child, I planned on being married, or in a happy, *committed* relationship at least, with someone who loved me and wanted to spend his life with me. So this is not the way I imagined it happening—separate homes, separate bedrooms, separate lives, with our child being shuffled back and forth between us. This is not what I wanted it to be.'

Damon was silent after she'd finished speaking, his fingers tapping out a slow beat on the table. Then, 'Carrie, even if there wasn't the obvious elephant in the room between us, I'm not sure it could be like that. I don't have long-term relationships. They're not what I want. And all you and I shared was one night.'

She held up a hand—a silent plea for him to stop. 'Its fine, Damon, I get it. I'm aware that what we had was just a one-night thing—just as I'm aware that Randolphs and Meyers are right up there with the Montagues and Capulets for families who shouldn't be together. I wasn't asking for the impossible. I just wanted to explain that this is hard for me too. Please don't misunderstand—I'm happy that you want to be involved, and we will find a way to make this work, but it is, nonetheless, hard.' She sucked in a sharp breath. 'One day I *will* find what I'm looking for. For now, I just need to adjust.'

She pushed back her chair, keeping hold of it as she pressed herself to her feet on legs that trembled.

'Thank you for dinner.'

His startled eyes followed her sudden upward movement. 'You're leaving? You've barely eaten anything.'

The last thing Carrie wanted to do was eat. Her stomach was twisted up in knots and the beats of her heart felt more like throbs.

Because she craved something that could never be. Belonging to a happy family unit had always been her dream, and when her parents' marriage had fallen apart she had directed all her hopes to the future…to the family she would build with the man of her dreams. She'd never lost that fantasy, not even after Nate. It had been a comfort to her, something she'd clung to as a promise of better days to come.

And even though she'd known there could never be anything more with Damon, her feelings for him had anchored deep from the moment they'd met, and because of that there had been a tiny kernel of hope that somehow…maybe…

But no! She had been foolish to allow that fantasy to build, and going forward she needed to maintain better control over her heart and her head. Going forward she needed to think of Damon only as exactly what he was—the father of her child. Nothing more.

'I'm all talked out and pretty tired—it's been a long day. But I'll see you tomorrow at the scan.' She spared him a brief glance as she hooked her bag over her shoulder. 'Goodnight.'

Damon rose to follow Carrie as she hastened to the door, his fists clenching as the impulse to reach out, catch her hand and stop her became stronger than the voice in his head screaming constant reminders that she was Sterling Randolph's daughter.

But what good would come from doing that? he thought irritably. Stop her and then… what, exactly?

She was a romantic. She craved the promise of a fairy-tale. He could not offer the words she so longed to hear, nor the future she'd pinned her hopes on. Even if she wasn't a Randolph his offerings would be limited. Relationships created an ever-present threat of loss and pain, neither of which he wanted. Therefore he could not act on the impulse heating his blood and making his heart thunder. It would be unfair to her.

He heard the door shut and stopped, cursing beneath his breath. Releasing a stressed huff of air, Damon wandered back out to the patio, looking up at the darkening sky and making every attempt to breathe through the longing that fogged up his head, to reorganise his thoughts into the correct order.

But ever since laying eyes on Carrie earlier that afternoon he'd thought of only one thing—losing himself in her once again. And every time he'd looked at her since, taking in the glossy waterfall of her ink-black hair, her luminous skin and glowing eyes and full lips—*those damnably kissable lips*—his mind had run wild with thoughts of surrendering himself to the delights of her body, to feeling how she arched beneath him as he found her sweet spot, to teasing her smooth skin with nips of his teeth and swipes of his tongue.

At one point it had become so unbearable he had been seconds away from shoving the table aside and pulling her out of her seat and into his arms. Only the last echoes of self-control had stopped him. Because he simply could not permit himself to do that. Taking her to bed once had been an act of betrayal. To do so again would be an even greater treachery.

Just because she was now carrying his heir, it didn't change what they could be.

It just complicated it.

Because now, for the sake of his child, he *needed* to have a relationship with her.

His own childhood had been gloriously happy. He had been safe in the love of both his parents and the stability of their solid, faithful marriage. He wanted his child to know something as close to that as possible, and his plan to co-parent should ensure that. Carrie had already shown that she would do what was best for their child, but he wondered suddenly and startlingly if she would continue to be amenable to that arrangement once his plan to ruin Randolph had succeeded.

By her own admission she and her father did not share a close relationship, but she seemed to have some tender feelings for the man, so how would she react to her father's downfall and Damon's role in it? His stomach lurched as, for the first time, he considered the possibility that she might reconsider his involvement in their child's life because of his actions.

The thought sat like a rock in his gut, even as he dismissed it as impossible. Carrie was not like his mother, who'd ignored his needs and flitted off with a new man to a new life that had no room for him. Carrie would put the needs and best interests of their child first, even if she was annoyed with him.

Wouldn't she?

Then, with another lurch, he recalled Carrie's words about one day finding a man to share her life with, and angry, scorching flames licked up the back of his throat. The thought of her lying in the arms of another man…of that same faceless nameless impostor taking his place in her life, in his child's life…

But wasn't it inevitable? Carrie was young, beautiful, vital. She deserved a loving partner. What right did he have to resent the future she would one day find when he was offering nothing? When he had nothing within him to offer.

His throat tightened painfully.

When in a matter of weeks she would learn of the demise of her father's business and that Damon was the man responsible...

Damon glanced at the clock hanging above the door in the doctor's office. He'd slept fitfully, tossing from one side of the king-sized bed to the other. When he hadn't been tortured by carnal dreams of Carrie's perfect form rising up and covering his body, he'd been tormented by more dark thoughts of what would happen to his relationship with Carrie and the baby when his revenge on her father was complete.

As a result his mood was black, and waiting for their appointment to start in this airless room where his every breath was infused with the scent of Carrie was making it blacker. With his chest uncomfortably tight and his heart pumping as if he was running a marathon, he felt more on edge than ever, and was willing the appointment to start just so it could end and he could return to Los Angeles and be free of the constant temptation of Carrie Miller.

Finally, the door of the screening room

swung open and a tall woman in her mid to late forties with fluffy blonde hair and a confident air walked in, aiming a smile first at Carrie and then at Damon. It went unreturned.

'Sorry to be a few moments late. I'm Elizabeth, your sonographer. You must be Carrie…' As she spoke she took a seat on the stool at the foot of the bed Carrie was reclined upon. 'And you must be the father?' She looked expectantly up at him.

'Damon Meyer,' he introduced himself tersely, speaking through the lurch of his stomach that had accompanied the word 'father.'

'Good to meet you. Do either of you have any questions before we start?' she enquired pleasantly.

They both shook their heads and with a glance between them she smiled, a knowingness shining in her expression. 'First baby?' When they nodded, she smiled again. 'Let's not keep you in suspense any longer, then. Just watch the screen.'

She pushed up the sheet draped over Carrie's mid-section, baring her still-flat stomach, and Damon gritted his teeth together on a hiss of breath as the exposed curve of her waist prompted bursts of tantalising memory.

His lips had kissed that dip as he'd mapped her body with his mouth. His hands had shaped that very curve as she had sat astride him.

As the throb in his groin was reignited, he blanked the heady images from his mind and watched as gel was squeezed onto Carrie's stomach and then spread across her skin with a wand.

The screen filled with a surprisingly clear black and white image, and with her finger Elizabeth pointed to a small peanut shape in the lower left corner of the image. 'This is your baby.'

'It's so tiny...' Carrie breathed.

'Just for now!' Elizabeth laughed. 'Would you like to hear the heartbeat?'

Delight lit Carrie's face, and as she nodded eagerly Elizabeth twisted one of the dials on the machine beneath the screen.

And that was when it happened. The steady, rhythmic pound of a tiny beating heart filled the room and everything in Damon shifted upright in recognition.

That was the sound of *his* child. His child's beating heart.

'Oh, wow.' Carrie pressed a hand to her mouth, an abundance of love shining in her eyes. 'That's incredible. Don't you think that's amazing?' She beamed at him, angling her face to where he stood.

Unable to move, and with his amazed eyes fixed on the screen, Damon could only nod. Because as he looked at this first image of his child, and listened to its strong and steady heartbeat, it was not the roiling dread that he had expected to feel churning in his gut, nor that old familiar fear of love and loss, but something entirely different. Something brilliantly warm and wondrous. Something that lifted him up and made his chest feel like an inflated balloon, suffused with so much joy he feared it might explode.

And the longer he looked and listened, the more incredible he felt. Because there, in the middle of the darkness of the screen, was a tiny spot of bright white light, like a star in a storm, beckoning him on and guiding him home.

CHAPTER SEVEN

CARRIE HAD JUST heard her baby's heart beating and it had been the most extraordinary
moment, wiping clear all the sadness that
had settled in her bones after the previous
evening's dinner with Damon and filling her
with more love than she'd ever felt before.

She was still marvelling at the life that was
growing inside her, so she didn't register the
ringing of her phone until Damon prompted her.

'It's probably just my mom, wanting to
know that everything with the baby is okay.'
She lifted the device to her ear, wiping away
the moisture beneath her eyes. 'Hi, Mom.
Guess what I just heard?'

'Sweetheart, don't panic, okay?'

Don't panic. Were there any words more
likely to cause panic?

The joy she had been revelling in was
numbed by a rush of foreboding. 'Why? What's
happened?'

Across the room, she saw Damon lift his eyes, alerted by her tone.

'It seems that a picture of you and Damon in Paris has emerged from somewhere. There are photographers outside my house right now, and outside your house and the bakery.'

Oh, God.

Panic closed its hands around her throat and set her heart racing like a runaway train.

'I don't think you should go back to your house, Carrie.'

'Where should I go, then?' she croaked. 'Grandma and Grandpa's?'

Prue hesitated. 'It will only be a matter of time before they make the connection and show up there too.'

The phone began to shake. It took Carrie a second to realise that it was her hand that was trembling, not the phone.

'I cannot believe this is happening,' she moaned, covering her eyes with her hand. 'I can't go through this again, Mom.'

'Sweetheart, just breathe.'

Carrie did as her mother told her, clinging to the calming familiarity of her voice.

'You can get through this. It will be all right.'

'What is it? What's wrong?'

Damon's sharp voice cut through the air

and she uncovered her eyes, but all she could make out was his blurry outline towering over her.

'Carrie?'

Impatience made his voice a harsh rasp against her tender senses and she flinched.

'It's… I…'

But she couldn't form the words, couldn't find enough air to take a breath. All she could think about was the mayhem that was waiting for her outside the four walls she was currently surrounded by.

'Carrie, give Damon the phone. Let me speak to him,' her mother instructed, and without another thought she held the phone out to Damon, who took it with a sceptical glance.

His eyes narrowed as he listened, his jaw hardening to such a degree she thought it could have cut through glass as easily as a knife through butter, but he held his composure—a feat that to Carrie seemed superhuman as she continued to shake so badly it wouldn't have surprised her if she'd actually started to crack apart.

'No, you're completely right,' he said finally. 'Being here right now is not a good idea, especially if we don't want them learning about the pregnancy. I'll take care of it. I know a place

Carrie and I can go to lie low. No, I'll tell her. It will be a few hours, but we will let you know when we get there. Okay. Bye.'

Pocketing her phone, Damon didn't waste a second before springing into determined action. 'We need to get out of here. Now.' He picked up his possessions and quickly checked outside the window. 'Come on.'

Carrie heard the urgency in his voice and knew she needed to move. Only she couldn't. She was frozen.

'Carrie…'

The hand that curled around her cheek was strong and warm, its touch so tender that she felt herself leaning into it, sinking into the reassurance and security it offered. Damon was crouching to her level, his luxuriant dark eyes boring into hers, burning all the way down to her toes, burning through the fear and making it easier for her to breathe the longer she looked into that beautiful gaze.

'We need to leave. I will keep you safe, but we have to go *now*. I need you to trust me.'

Trust me.

He was asking for the impossible, but as his gaze held hers in a silent promise she felt herself nodding. He clasped her hand and gently pulled her to her feet, steering her out through the door. He didn't let go all the way out of the clinic and to his car, like a solid anchor keeping her steady.

He put her in the car, helped her pull the seatbelt across her weak and trembling body, and within minutes they were speeding down the freeway, out of Santa Barbara. By that time Carrie had regained some of her equilibrium, though she was still frightened and darting her eyes out through the back window to see if they were being followed.

'It's okay. There's no one following us.'

Damon didn't take his eyes off the road ahead as he offered his reassurance, and the speedometer was racing upwards at a frightening speed.

'Are you sure?'

He nodded, deftly darting into the neighbouring lane on the freeway, his strong, tanned hands steady on the wheel. 'I have some experience with this.'

'So do I,' Carrie muttered, twisting her hands together in her lap, an action she knew his alert eyes didn't miss even as she quickly pulled them apart and wedged them beneath her legs.

'Are you okay?'

Carrie glanced at him and then quickly looked away, scared that everything she was feeling, every ounce of her fragility, would be visible in her expression.

'What did my mother tell you?'

'That you suffer from panic attacks.'

Carrie stiffened. 'It's one of those things that sounds worse than it is,' she asserted, with a defensiveness she couldn't help. 'It's not a constant thing. I just have flare-ups in certain situations.'

'I'm not judging you, Carrie,' he said. 'I brought it up just to see if you were okay, so you could tell me if you're…struggling. So I can help.'

'I've been worse.'

'But you've also been better,' he stated, reading what she hadn't said. 'When did you start having the panic attacks?'

Crossing her arms, she directed her stare straight ahead, resenting that she had been thrust into a situation that demanded she share any of this with him. The last thing she wanted to do was open herself up to him. Secrets and scars were meant to be shared with those who loved you, and that definitely wasn't Damon. He'd made that clear the night before, and Carrie had spent the past twelve hours drilling it into herself how important it was that she guarded herself from him emotionally.

He was the father of her child, nothing more. They needed to be amicable, nothing more. Yet she could tell by the expectant silence that he would wait as long as necessary to get an answer.

'When I was eight,' she relented eventually.

'*Eight?*' he repeated, astonished colour darkening the line of his cheekbones. 'What could have possibly happened when you were that young to—?'

He broke off as his mind completed the calculation and came to the obvious conclusion. To the one thing their relationship always came back to.

'The scandal.'

Carrie watched his knuckles glow white as his hands tensed around the steering wheel.

'What happened?' he asked.

'Life went crazy. Everyone wanted a piece of my father…our family. Every time we set foot outside, the press swarmed. Basic trips to school and the shops became an ordeal. We were followed, photographed incessantly, screamed at on a daily basis. It was horrific.'

Even speaking about it brought it too close, and she momentarily closed her eyes to block out the memories.

'For me it became debilitating—our faces all over the papers, everybody watching us and talking about us. That's when the panic attacks started. I was too frightened to leave the house. I stopped going to school. It was the main reason my mom moved us back to California during the divorce.'

She suppressed a shiver, the memory leaving her chilled to the bone.

'I never want to go through that kind of insanity again.'

Inhaling deeply, and reminding herself that in this moment she was safe, she tried to focus on the landscape flying past the window. It was only then that Carrie realised she had no idea where Damon was taking her.

'Where are we going?' she demanded, with a turn of her head.

'Ojai. It's about an hour outside of LA.'

'Why there?'

'I have a home there,' he answered crisply. 'I lived there for some of my childhood.'

Carrie kept her expression neutral even as her pulse jerked. He was taking her to *his house*? She wasn't so sure she liked the sound of that. She needed to be somewhere she could feel safe and calm—and he made her feel neither of those things.

And then an even more unpleasant thought occurred. 'Does your mother still live in Ojai?'

'No,' he responded after a brief hesitation. 'My mother never lived there.'

Carrie chewed on her lip in confusion. 'But you...you said you lived there for some of your childhood...'

'My father was from Ojai. When he was alive we visited often. But I went to live there full-time after he died, with my father's sister, my aunt Bree, and her family.'

'Why didn't you stay with your mother?' Carrie probed, peering at him more closely and noting the way his jaw was clenched, as though his memories were hard to contend with.

'She remarried very quickly and relocated to Europe,' he replied. She saw a nerve beginning to pulse in that solid jaw. 'She felt that, given everything that had happened with my father, it would be better for me to stay here, with his family. That it would be too much upheaval for me to leave.'

He was trying to paint a civilised picture of what had transpired, but Carrie was not fooled. She could see the ugly truth of it.

'She sent you away from her?' she gasped disbelievingly.

Judging others was not something Carrie liked to do—not after the way she had been scrutinised and judged just for being her father's daughter, over and over again, and goodness knew Damon and his mother's lives had been turned upside down with the sudden death of Jacob. But to willingly separate from her child at a time when he'd needed her most…

Carrie knew there was no universe in which her mother would fail to be there for her. Prue Miller had always put Carrie first, uprooting her whole life to safeguard her daughter. And, although she did not know her baby yet, Carrie could not foresee any hardship being so great that she would part from her precious child.

'It wasn't quite that stark or simple,' Damon expressed with a bite of irritation, his darkening gaze still fixed resolutely ahead. 'My father had lived to make her happy. He'd handled everything. She was cherished and insulated. But everything surrounding his death was so ugly that it was too much for her. She wanted to still be insulated, and she found someone who could give her that.'

'But you needed to be protected and insulated too,' insisted Carrie. 'You were just a boy.'

His admission the previous night that he had no desire for a long-term relationship had left her stunned, but it was little wonder after he'd learned at a young age that relationships offered no guarantee of for ever. How could he trust in any woman to stay by his side when his mother had so easily left him behind? How could she have treated him that way?

He glanced across at her and, expecting some kind of rebuke, Carrie was startled when those spectacular planes of his face that were always so hard in his regard of her softened, smoothing into something that edged towards tenderness.

'You're going to be a good mom, Carrie.'

Amazed, she could only stare back at him, trying to fathom what had prompted the high compliment and wishing he had not issued it. Because it had caused feelings she didn't want to feel for him to fizz in her stomach and at the apex of her thighs. Feelings which only intensified as his eyes turned molten with a sensual golden gleam.

Her bones shook. Heat swelled between them, surrounding them, and at once Carrie was aware of a tingling in her breasts, and the way her nipples were hardening into tight and begging buds.

Furious with how quickly she had fallen under his spell, she pulled her gaze away.

'I'm tired… I may just close my eyes for a little while,' she said, staring straight ahead but seeing nothing as waves of traitorous heat continued to crash through her.

'That's a good idea,' Damon agreed, clearing his throat. 'We'll be on the road for another hour or so.'

She turned her face away, bewildered that the glitter of his eyes had been enough of an invitation to send her body spinning out of control. It was exactly what she had instructed herself *not* to let happen!

Refusing to dwell on it any longer, Carrie slammed her eyes shut, determined to put him out of her head. But in the dreamscape of her mind Damon was waiting, and in his eyes was that intoxicating golden shimmer, and when he reached out to touch her she did absolutely nothing to resist him…

As he slowed the car to a stop at a red light, Damon took his eyes off the road to glance beside him at Carrie's sleeping form. Her chest moved gently up and down, her feathery lashes brushed the skin beneath her eyes and her deep pink lips were pressed firmly together.

She was so achingly beautiful that once it was on her he could not tear his gaze away. Nor did he want to look away. He was happy to simply stare at her, remembering how it had felt to be seated deep inside her, how she had come to life in his arms when he'd crushed those velvet-soft lips beneath his own. Each time he looked at her, feeling that all-over tug of urgent desire, he felt the will to resist doing so again eroded a little more.

He'd never known anything like it. He was used to liking a woman, pursuing her or responding to her pursuit of him, enjoying a brief, fun-filled affair and then walking away. Never had he been tempted to prolong any of those interactions. Never had he craved more. He'd never felt a *need* for a woman, as if she was critical to his survival. He'd never been physically incapable of drawing his eyes away.

With her it was different.

But everything was different with her.

She made him consider a different life... the pursuit of other priorities. Like family. Partnership. Love.

All the things that he had closed himself off from after his father had been killed and his mother had turned away.

All the things he'd decided he didn't want because they posed too great a risk.

But for reasons he didn't understand around her they felt...*possible.*

The sharp blast of a horn at his rear prodded him back to his senses and, seeing the light had turned to green, he slammed his foot down on the accelerator and zoomed forward, now less than ten miles from the last place he had expected to find himself.

Damon retained his home in Ojai because the house was a connection to his father, a piece of his inheritance, but it was a bittersweet place for him. A place with a thousand happy memories of life *before* and a thousand bleak memories of life *after*.

But it was a location very few people knew to associate with him, making it a safe place for Carrie, and that was the most important thing—especially after seeing the fear that had overridden her every defence, infiltrating every inch of her until she was cold to the touch.

Damon had had no idea she had suffered so much in the aftermath of the scandal. He'd been so preoccupied with his own pain and what he'd lost it had never occurred to him—not even in the time since—that the scandal had created numerous victims, inflicted untold suffering.

At the first test it seemed he'd lost sight of all the lessons his father had worked to instil in him—consideration, empathy and understanding.

Just like his mother, he had been selfish in his grief.

For that, he was ashamed of himself. Ashamed that he'd been so blind and thoughtless. Ashamed that he'd not acted like his father, or the man his father would have expected him to be. Ashamed of the way he'd taken every opportunity to bludgeon Carrie with the hurt of his past when the whole time she had been carrying around her own burden of hurt.

But now he knew and he would be better.

Starting with Carrie. He would protect her the way she should have been protected as a child. As far as he was concerned it was one more crime to add to Randolph's docket that he had failed to ensure his daughter's physical and emotional wellbeing, and it made his blood bubble with fury. But *he* would not fail her. He would keep her safe, doing all in his power to ensure she was never made to suffer again—by the press, by her father, or by himself.

But even as he made that vow a voice in his head questioned how he would keep it.

His actions of revenge would guarantee that their families were swept up in a new media storm, and no amount of hired security could protect her from the trauma of that.

Nor would he be able to protect Carrie from the pain of seeing her father's life in ruins. And what of the pain she would endure when she realised *he'd* been the architect of it all?

Randolph deserved everything that was heading his way. *But,* that voice in his head demanded, *if you also cause Carrie pain with your actions, are you any better than her father?*

CHAPTER EIGHT

OJAI HAD TO be one of the most beautiful places on earth, Carrie thought, as she admired yet another spectacular view from yet another window of Damon's home, this one stretching towards the mountains. Standing on the terrace of the guest room designated to her, she grazed her eyes over the majestic scenery, breathing in the scent of rosemary and lemon blossom as a soft breeze kissed her face.

She had just been stirring when they had arrived at the town limits, and although her sleep had been fraught with dreams of Damon and nameless figures chasing her, waking to the quaint and rustic glamour of Ojai had made her spirits lighter.

Then Damon had steered the car along a very quiet road, turning in at a set of high carved iron gates and following a brick driveway. And there, nestled amongst the abundant greenery of trees and hedges, had been the most beautiful villa. With bright white walls, terracotta roofs, and the trickle of a fountain hidden amongst the lush and colourful garden.

Carrie had loved the oasis on first sight, and inside had proved just as beautiful, remaining true to its Spanish colonial style with tiled ceilings, white walls and a flowing and open concept.

Damon had spared just enough time to give her a quick tour and show her to a bedroom before taking a call from his assistant and issuing instructions to postpone and rearrange scheduled meetings. That had been over forty minutes ago, and she hadn't seen him since—which was hardly surprising, given that she was probably the last woman on earth he wanted to share his home with.

Whilst Carrie was grateful she hadn't been alone to manage her panic when she'd received that call from her mom back at the clinic, and was even more grateful that Damon's quick thinking had allowed them to escape unscathed, being far from home and an unwanted house guest was hardly ideal.

Carrie was still lost in those bleak thoughts when she was startled by a noise behind her.

Twisting her head over her shoulder, she felt her heart jerk to see Damon in the open doorway.

'You settling in okay?' he asked with an easy smile.

She nodded, wishing he was asking because he cared and not because she was his responsibility by virtue of the baby she carried.

'My assistant has arranged for a selection of clothes and personal products and whatever else she thinks you may need to be delivered.'

'Thanks.'

But she was struggling to make her answering smile stick to her lips and Damon noticed it, surveying her with concern.

'What's the matter? Are you still feeling anxious?'

'No. I feel a lot better than I did. I just… I feel bad you had to get involved,' she admitted uncomfortably. 'I overheard the start of your call with your assistant…organising how to rearrange your meetings. I've completely upended your life with this.'

He advanced towards her, his body seeming more powerful, more commanding, in the casual attire of black jeans and a black tee.

'You haven't upended anything. Technology being what it is today means I can have meetings any time, anywhere.'

His kindness was unexpected, and his words sounded sincere, but they did little to expunge her feelings of guilt.

'Really, don't worry about it.'

'I just can't help but think that if I'd told you who I was straight away, none of this would be happening right now,' she blurted out.

Damon stilled, his eyes creasing at the corners. 'Is that what you wish you had done?'

'Yes.'

Because then her life wouldn't be under attack for a second time by a horde of paparazzi. Nor would she be a burden to a man who didn't want to spend time with her and whom she was loath to trust too much in case her trust was misplaced—*again*. On the other hand, if she had been honest with him they would probably not have shared that magical night together, and she wouldn't trade those memories for anything. And she also wouldn't be carrying his child.

The thought of that parallel world made her queasy.

'No,' she amended quickly, regretting her outburst and knowing that even if the chance was offered to go back in time and do it differently, she wouldn't. 'No, it's not. I just wish everything wasn't such a mess.'

'It's not a mess. The furore over this picture will die down. The press will find a new story to pick apart and they'll forget all about us. And until then you're safe here.'

'And after that?' she asked, hugging her arms around herself and wishing it was *his* arms tucked tight around her. But that only made her nerves feel more frazzled. 'At some point it will get out that I'm pregnant, and that the baby's yours, and when it does…' Carrie couldn't even complete the sentence without feeling overwhelmed.

'We'll figure it out,' he was quick to assure her, injecting his voice with a steeliness that garnered her faith. 'Whatever it takes, I will keep you and our baby safe. I won't let you go through what you did as a child. I give you my word.'

With a single step he closed the space between them, and she felt a tug low in her stomach at his nearness.

'We are in this together.'

She had to tip her head back to look at him, and the look in his eye set her heart pounding. 'Do you really mean that?' she asked, so badly wanting to believe in the promise contained within his words and his gaze, but so accustomed to words carrying no more weight than air.

'Yes, I do.'

And then he made the most remarkable move, stunning her into stillness. Reaching out, Damon brushed a stray tendril of hair behind her ear, the tips of his fingers lingering against her cheek. Sparks cartwheeled though her as a dusting of gold exploded in his gaze. Scared to move or breathe, in case she broke the connection, she waited for his next move, willing him to make one, to offer some signal that he felt everything she did... that she wasn't imagining these moments of pure physical, sensual connection.

But then her phone chirped from her bag, where she had dropped it on the floor, shattering the moment. Damon dropped his hand and with a sigh Carrie reached down to extract the offending item, her features growing taut as she checked the display.

After a brief hesitation, in which her finger hovered indecisively, she rejected the call.

'Who was that?' Damon enquired, eyes sharp.

'Jonathan. My brother.'

The phone rang again. Carrie took one look and jabbed it so it fell silent.

'And Wren. Obviously they've seen the headlines today. No doubt Xander will be next.'

Anxiety advancing once more, she collapsed onto the edge of the bed, dropping her head into her hands. She loved her half-brothers, but she wasn't sure she had the energy to give them the fight they were calling to have. She already knew they'd be furious with her. As ardent followers of their father, anything that displeased him, displeased them.

The phone rang again. Xander, as predicted.

'Exactly how big a problem are they going to have with this?'

Carrie raised her gaze to Damon. 'With the rumours about you and I? A pretty big one.'

'Which you knew would be the case,' he ascertained from her expression. 'And yet you still came to the party? To me?'

Carrie held her breath. She had risked her relationship with her brothers and her father that night in Paris, knowing that if they ever found out about any flirtation between her and Damon they would be uncompromising in their anger. But she'd been desperate to see him one more time.

Now Damon knew that too. And it caused her stomach to drop away. Because all she wanted was to protect herself, protect her heart, and yet he seemed to be accessing more and more of her.

A look so fleeting she had no time to de-cipher it shot across his eyes like a shooting star. He kept on looking at her, and she was powerless to do anything but gaze right back at him until her phone buzzed once again.

Not bothering to glance at the caller ID, she sighed. 'I should answer. They won't stop until I do.'

'Do you want me to talk to them?' Damon offered, making no move to leave.

'I think that would be the equivalent of pouring oil onto a fire. It's better if I deal with them.'

'Then I'll give you some privacy.'

With seeming reluctance he walked to the door, leaving Carrie with the impression that he didn't really want to leave her. But that was unlikely, wasn't it? Because he definitely didn't want to spend any more time with her than he had to.

But what about his promise to protect her, and that tender caress of her face…?

Her heart tripped at thinking about it again.

However, as her phone rang again, with more insistence, she put those thoughts aside, raised it to her ear and took a deep breath.

Damon retreated to the seclusion of his office and forced himself to remain there and not dwell on the conversation happening upstairs that was technically none of his business. He made himself sit at his desk and go through his emails, respond to the most urgent. To review plans. To sketch.

Even when he heard the gentle patter of her feet descending the stairs, and his body reacted with exhilaration, he made himself stay still, stay seated. To remain distant and detached even if it was only a physical distance, because he'd failed to remain emotionally disconnected.

When his nose detected scents of something mouth-watering being concocted by her talented hands, he battled the compulsion to go to her, to just be near her. Because he couldn't. Or, more accurately, he shouldn't. And he certainly shouldn't want to.

Yet he did, and none of the distractions he'd employed had succeeded in quelling that want, or in dimming his awareness of her being just a few metres away.

When, with a tentative knock, she appeared in his doorway, Damon devoured the sight of her, his hands curled into fists around the sides of his chair because he did not trust himself not to fly from his seat, pin her delicious body against the nearest wall and feast on her.

Despite the trauma of the day, and the strain hugging her eyes, she looked as beautiful as she had first thing that morning. So much had happened in the past ten hours. So much in his own mind had shifted and become uncertain.

'I'm not disturbing you, am I?' she asked, when he didn't immediately speak.

'No. How did the conversation with your brothers go?'

'About as unpleasantly as expected.' She shrugged her shoulders up to her chin. 'They were furious and they had lots of questions, which was not helped by my telling them that how I spend my time and with whom is not their business. They said I was being disloyal...that you have some vendetta against our father because of...everything.'

Damon stilled, his pulse stalling. 'I'm sorry it didn't go well.'

Carrie shook her head, brushing off his concern even though he could see she was troubled. 'I've made some food. I thought you might want to come and eat.'

He definitely wanted to devour her...all of her...very, *very* slowly. But since that was the last thing he should do...

'I'm not all that hungry, but thank you.'

Moving deeper into the study, she stood

right on the other side of the desk, which suddenly seemed far too narrow. She was so close that with every breath he was catching the scent of her shampoo—something soft and calming. He had been hit by it earlier, in the bedroom, and once more the scent propelled his mind back to their night together and how, even as he'd half slept, he'd been conscious of that scent, using the arm anchored around her waist to pull her closer, so he could bury his face even more deeply against her fall of dark hair...

'Damon, my guess is you've not eaten since breakfast. If you're going to work for hours on end, then you need sustenance. So come on... I'm not taking no for an answer. Consider it a thank-you for all you've done today.'

'All right.' Catching himself smiling at her insistence, he got to his feet and walked in silence with her to the kitchen where the most delicious aromas swirled in the air, tempting his stomach. 'How many people were you actually cooking for?' he asked, seeing everything her busy hands had made.

The laugh that escaped her lips was self-conscious, but oh-so-sexy. 'I know... I went a little overboard. But whenever I feel anxious or stressed I cook,' she confided. 'It was my grandmother who started it. When the anxiety attacks were at their worst, she thought if I had something to focus my mind on it would help me take back control of my body. She was right. Measuring out ingredients, working through recipes, all that stirring and kneading… It helped me channel my energy and calm down. And it felt so good I wanted to spend all my time doing it.'

She had plated up their food as she talked, and it was only as she sat down that she looked at Damon's expression as he took his first mouthful.

'You don't like it?'

He swallowed. 'It's delicious. I don't think I've ever tasted anything so good, and I've eaten in some fairly high-end restaurants.' He sampled another forkful. 'Your talents are *not* limited to baking. With food this good you could be running a five-star kitchen.'

'Restaurant hours are a nightmare. And they wouldn't fit in very well with caring for a baby.'

'Is that why you didn't become a chef? The hours?' he queried, because he couldn't see what else had stopped her.

'Actually, when I first left cookery school I figured my path would take me to a restaurant. And I was actually offered a job as a pastry chef.'

'What happened?'

The light in her face dimmed. 'I very quickly learned that I'd only been offered the job because of who my father was.' Her eyes travelled up to his. 'The chef wanted to ensure her new restaurant was a success. She thought hiring me would earn the patronage of my father and all his wealthy acquaintances.'

'You wouldn't be the first person to get a job because of nepotism,' he pointed out.

'No, but it's not how I wanted to get that job—or any job. It's not how I wanted to live my life...always having to wonder if I was good enough or if I just had the right name. I wanted to earn it...to be the best. I wanted that job because there was no one else who could do it as well as I could. Not because I was someone's daughter.'

He heard her resentment and for the first time realised what a weight her father's name and reputation must have been to shoulder. 'And that's why you changed your name?'

She nodded. 'I just want to be able to be myself, to be free. I don't want to always have a target on my back. To always wonder if it's about me or my name.'

Damon frowned at her aggressive phrasing. *A target on her back?* 'The person who hurt you…the one you mentioned to me in Paris…that was to do with your name, too, wasn't it?'

'Yes.'

She fidgeted, making it clear she did not want to unlock that box of memories, and for that reason Damon knew that whatever happened had been bad—because she was inherently open. He saw that about her now. Saw how difficult she must have found it to know she had not been telling him the whole truth about herself.

'Let me get you more risotto,' she said.

Grabbing her wrist as she tried to rise, he prevented her from running away. 'You can either tell me yourself, or with a quick call I can have someone else find me the information,' he said, gentling the threat with a softer than usual tone.

Her agitation skipped up a few levels. 'Why do you even want to know? Why does it matter?'

'Because we're having a child together, and that necessitates us knowing certain things about each other.'

At least that was the convenient explanation. In fact, his desire to know was a lot deeper and simpler than that. He wanted to know. Wanted to know *her*. Her hurts, her bruises, her scars, her hopes and fears. He wanted to know everything.

Carrie sent him an arch look. 'Yet when I asked about your mother leaving you, *you* were not very forthcoming. Why should I share with you when you won't with me?'

Touché.

'I don't know how to talk about what happened with my mother,' he confessed, steeling himself for the searing pain that accompanied any thought or words about her. 'My father died and it broke her heart. I understand that. But the choices she made afterwards—to remarry so quickly, to send me here—I don't understand. I'd like to think that she did what she did because she thought it was in my best interests, but I'm not sure I believe that.'

'Do you ever see her?'

'She and my stepfather live in the South of France. She comes to the States maybe once a year. We have lunch.'

'Lunch?' she repeated, bewildered.

He nodded solemnly, struck again by the realisation that Carrie was as different from his own mother as it was possible to be.

She sighed. 'His name was Nate. The person who hurt me. He worked for my father and he was ambitious. He saw me as a way he could progress faster. I thought he was charming and kind. I'd always liked the idea of my own fairy-tale, so the thought that he'd fallen madly in love with me at first sight was intoxicating. But then he didn't get a promotion that he wanted, so he went to my father and attempted to blackmail him. He said he had photos of me that he would take to the press, along with details of our relationship, if he wasn't given an executive position.'

She paused, twisting her fingers together, her plate of food forgotten.

'He said he loved me, but all along he'd only cared about himself. I was just a means to an end.' Giving a tiny shake of her head, she pressed her eyes shut as though the simple act would erase it. 'I was so stupid not to see it.'

'No, Carrie.' Damon hurried to reassure her, hating it that she blamed herself for even a second. 'People like that are very good at what they do. *You* are not stupid.'

It was then that he saw the glisten of tears in her eyes.

'My father didn't see it that way. He was so angry that I'd exposed him and his business to humiliation. I'd always known his work mattered more to him than anything, that everyone else came second to the Randolph Corporation, but knowing it and seeing it are two very different things. And that was the day I saw it. My heartbreak and humiliation didn't even hit his radar. He didn't even ask if I was okay.'

'That's why you don't have a relationship with him?' Damon asked quietly, suddenly realising their faces were only inches apart. Without his noticing, their bodies had inched closer together, their knees brushing beneath the table.

Carrie nodded sadly. 'I wanted to be close with him so badly. When I was younger and he didn't show up I told myself not to be hurt, that he was a busy man…he did important work. Then Nate happened. All I wanted was to know that he cared about me, but the only thing he cares about in life is business and success. It's all that matters to him. All he sees.'

Damon's gut twisted, because he knew the same ugly accusation could be levelled against him, and in the past it had been. It was a comparison that had his stomach writhing and bile climbing up his throat. Because if there was one man on earth he didn't want to be like, it was Sterling Randolph. A man who had respect for nothing and nobody except the almighty dollar. And it was the second time that day he'd realised he might be more like him than he cared for.

'The truth is my father doesn't have relationships. He has the Randolph Corporation. That's his only meaningful relationship. And waiting for him to open his eyes and see you is like waiting for rain in a drought.' She sighed, the sound carrying a lifetime of disappointment. 'And yet I still hope that one day he will open his eyes.'

'Why?'

Damon didn't bother to temper the harshness of his disbelief. He'd never been short on reasons to despise Randolph, but the way he had treated Carrie incited in him a fury that would have made the gods quake. So to hear her openly admit that she still harboured hopes of a reconciliation with the man was mind-blowing.

'It doesn't sound as though he's been any kind of a father to you.'

She lifted her shoulders in a small, non-defensive shrug. 'Because he is my father,' she supplied simply.

And, looking into her guileless gaze, he realised that it was that simple for her. In Carrie's view, no matter what sins he had committed, Randolph was her father, and that was a relationship she would always stand by with love and loyalty, even if it was unreturned. She was that open-hearted. That pure. Once she loved, she loved for ever. And that was a lot like *his* father. So like his father he felt a crippling twist of his gut.

'And because I understand why he is so infuriatingly single-minded...why he pours all of his energy and attention into the Randolph Corporation.'

'Why does he?' Damon asked after a beat. He was unsure if it was a sensible question to ask, but she'd piqued his interest.

'Because he grew up very poor. When his father died, my dad, as the oldest, got a job so the family wouldn't be homeless. He went to school in the daytime and worked at night at all of fourteen years old. Can you imagine that? Having the responsibility for your whole family on your shoulders when you're just a boy? Knowing that whether they eat that day depends on you?'

Carrie shuddered, and even Damon had to acknowledge the icy chill skating across his broad shoulders at the thought of such desolate circumstances.

'Eventually he dropped out of school entirely and worked full-time to take care of them. Even when he started his own company and began to make big money he never stopped taking care of them. So everything he's managed to achieve in his life is incredible. And I think he believes that if he takes his eyes off it, even for a second, it will all disappear. I think that fear is what drives a lot of his actions. It hurts me, but I think it's understandable.'

Damon reached for his water glass, taking a long swallow. His throat felt like sandpaper.

This was information he'd never had any desire to know. Damon had made it his business to learn everything about Randolph's business affairs, but the finer details of his life had held zero interest. It had been enough to know that the man had brought about his father's death, and seeing him like that, in black and white, had suited him just fine.

But the particulars Carrie had just revealed shaded him in colour. It was hard to align the man who had endlessly provided for his family with the villain who had traded his father's life for a greater profit, and it was hard not to feel some admiration for the man who had built his empire from dirt and air.

And that strange new feeling, wedged like a thorn in his side, was giving him uncomfortable pause for thought, raising quiet questions, for the first time ever, over what would happen to the man once Damon had succeeded in bringing about his downfall. With those facts of his life pinballing around his mind, Damon knew his vengeance held not only the power to bring his empire crumbling to the ground, but to cripple the man who sat at its helm.

It should have been a satisfying feeling. A few months ago it would have steeped him in elation.

But now…it didn't.

And that disturbed him more than words could express. Because thinking of Sterling Randolph as a human being… *No!* He could not afford to start thinking of Randolph as a person if he was to defeat him…not now… not when he was so close.

'You show a lot of understanding. More than I would argue that he deserves,' Damon intoned, clawing back his anger.

'I think everyone deserves understanding and compassion.'

'Everyone?' Her sentiment struck a flame to the emotions kindling within him and he eyed her with dangerously simmering outrage. 'Is this your less than subtle way of telling me to let go of my anger towards him? To find *understanding and compassion*?'

'What…?' Bewilderment clouded her expression. 'No. Of course not. I'm just… We're talking… I was speaking for myself… I—'

'Because that is never going to happen, Carrie,' he exploded, his breaths heavy, his words loaded with a fury that was pressing against his chest like a bar of steel. 'What he did is unforgivable. There's no way back from that.'

Carrie's throat was so tight with emotion she could barely swallow, let alone speak, but after a long moment, punctured only by Damon's furiously ragged breaths, the question tearing at her emerged.

'Is this how it's always going to be?'

Her voice was small and quiet, but the stare she directed at Damon commanded an answer.

'Everything I say, everything I do, you'll assume some ulterior Machiavellian motive?'

He looked away from her. His sharp cheekbones were ablaze with colour and a nerve pulsed in his jaw, but he made no effort to respond. And in that deafening and frigid silence Carrie knew she had her answer.

She pressed her lips together to lock in the cry of anguish that tore through her. Could she be any *more* stupid? She had thought something in him had softened towards her. She'd actually believed that over dinner and conversation they were forging a new connection. A tentative one, of course, but something new…something that was just about the two of them. But no, it could never be just about the two of them, could it? Damon would never *allow* it to be. His anger over the events two decades ago was anchored so deep in him that it spilled across all else like a flood of thick black oil.

Suddenly exhausted, drained by the effort of trying and hoping and being let down, Carrie scraped back her chair and pushed herself to her feet. She was no longer interested in hearing whatever answer he might concoct, or in waiting to hear it. Nor in giving him yet another chance.

The only consolation she could draw was that at least she now knew unequivocally where she stood. That pesky, hopeful part of her that was always waiting for the sunshine to break through the clouds had pushed her to hope that there could be more between them—even if only a friendship—that it might be possible for him to see her as Carrie the way she saw him as simply Damon. Not as the sum of his parts, or a victim of his past, or the face of his successes—just him. But no. Not possible after all.

Her eyes were well and truly open now, and the clarity was so bright it was blinding.

'Carrie…'

'Do not!' She pulled her whole body out of his reach as he followed her hasty retreat from the kitchen with a thudding stride. 'Do not touch me. Do not talk to me. Because no matter what you say it's never going to change. How you look at me…the way you see me. In your eyes I will never be anything more than his daughter.'

Even in that moment, even looking at him with exasperated eyes, Carrie thought how achingly beautiful he was. But all he ever saw was her father.

'The only thing I want you to do right now is to leave me alone. And stop pretending to care.'

Once again he made no response before she turned and launched herself up the stairs, firmly pressing the door to her room closed and resenting the lack of a lock on the door. Not that she thought he would make any attempt to come to her, but Carrie wanted to physically complete the action of locking herself safely away from him.

Realising that every inch of her was trembling, she set herself down on the edge of the bed and dragged a sheepskin throw around her shoulders. She fixed her gaze on the verdant valley beyond the window, and when she felt her hand was steady enough reached for the glass of water on the bedside table.

Hot, hateful tears scorched her eyes and rolled down her cheeks as the depth of her stupidity pierced her all over again. She had prised herself open and revealed to him her heart, her scars, her fears. And with that caustic reaction he had thrown her trust and vulnerability back at her. Would she never learn?

Carrie assumed he would apologise, the same way he had before. He would blame too many emotions, too much stress, maybe. But she didn't want another apology. She wanted him to be different, to be better.

And therein lay the problem.

She was waiting for him to be the man she'd met in Paris. Only that Damon didn't seem to exist. And she couldn't keep on waiting and hoping. Not again.

It was exactly what she'd done with her father—hoping and waiting for him to be a better man, a better father. A father who cared and who made time for her. She had waited and waited…and she was still waiting.

Carrie would not consent to subjecting herself to the same torment with Damon.

It might have felt like a fairy-tale when they'd met, but there was never going to be a fairy-tale ending for her and Damon.

CHAPTER NINE

IT WAS NO USE. Eyes wide, Carrie knew she wasn't going to achieve any more of the fitful pockets of sleep that she'd managed throughout the night, so she flipped back the covers, slid her feet from the bed and, trying to make no sound at all, crept across the floor and eased open the door.

Firing glances left and right, to make sure the corridor was clear, she tiptoed down the stairs, making for the kitchen in search of an activity to occupy her mind and her hands—the only activity that would satisfy in her state: baking.

But she came to an uncertain stop when she saw the kitchen was already occupied. The doors were pushed back entirely and Damon was leaning with one strong shoulder against the wall, his attention fixed on the horizon, where the sun was cresting the gentle slopes of the mountains.

Her heart thudding, Carrie started to retreat.

'Don't leave.'

She stopped, the words commanding her even though they were the very opposite of what she wanted to do.

'You don't need to leave.'

He turned as he spoke and the moment their eyes locked Carrie felt all the pain of the previous night weave through her afresh, but the impact was dimmed by the sight of something dark harrowing his expression.

'You're awake early.'

'I haven't been to sleep,' he admitted, eyes pinning her with their haunted darkness.

Carrie nodded and averted her gaze, walking towards the cupboards. 'I was thinking of making some breakfast, if you're hungry. Maybe pancakes. Or bagels.'

Opening a cupboard, she reached in and retrieved whatever her hands touched, too aware of Damon closing the distance between them to be able to concentrate. She didn't want him near her because she didn't know what she would do. The urge to slap him was very real, but so was the desire to sink against him, cling to his hard body and cry out all her pain.

'I know you don't want an apology,' he

began, sounding shaky and very unlike himself, 'but I want you to know that I *am* sorry for last night. For jumping to conclusions. And for hurting you.'

Tears pricked at her eyes. The words were kind, but as she had feared they were not enough. They weren't the words she wanted, nor the ones she needed.

'Let's just not dwell on it, okay?' she said, feeling exhausted at the thought of going round and round again and getting nowhere. 'It's not like it was anything new. Let's just focus on how we can work together for the good of our child.'

She was letting him off the hook, so she didn't understand why Damon's expression remained bleak, his shoulders pitched high with tension.

'But, like you said, it's there between us. Always.'

Crossing his arms over his chest, he dug his hands into his underarms and a ripple of foreboding shot through her.

'There are some things that I would like to tell you…to explain, if you're willing to listen.'

Carrie was only used to seeing him in supreme control, assured and solid, so that witnessing him on a lower vibration was unsettling. But it was clear that whatever was on his mind troubled him, and she wouldn't refuse him the opportunity to unburden himself. Nor would she deny herself the opportunity to maybe finally understand him better.

'I'll listen,' she said, meeting his eyes properly for the first time since entering the kitchen and feeling the expected shiver slither through her.

Damon gestured to the patio. 'Let's sit outside.'

Carrie instantly tensed at the thought of taking the same places they had the previous night, but Damon led her to a more casual seating space that overlooked the pool and towards the mountains.

As they both sat he leant forward, legs splayed, elbows balanced on his knees and his head bowed, as if physically burdened by whatever he was on the point of revealing. The forlorn sight hollowed out her stomach, and with a fretful leap Carrie's heart launched itself into her throat, its uneven beats escalating more the longer Damon went without speaking.

But whatever this was, she sensed that he needed to begin in his own time, when the right words came to him.

She only had to wait a few more minutes.

'The day everything happened in Chicago…the day my father died,' he began, looking down at the ground. 'I was there.'

'You were there?' she repeated, floored by the confession.

How had she not known that? Since meeting Damon she'd scoured through everything she could find about the scandal, wanting to know it all, attempting to understand him.

'Nothing I've ever read about that day said anything about you…'

'My family kept it out of the press and convinced the authorities to do the same. They thought I'd been traumatised enough, witnessing it, without my name being in all the papers and having reporters clamouring for my story,' he explained dully. 'But I thought you had a right to know. And after last night, the way I reacted to the mention of your father, I wanted you to know. So you could understand why I…why I reacted the way I did. The way I always do.'

Her skin chilled as the truth sank in. He had been there. He'd watched his father die.

'Why didn't you tell me this sooner?'

'I've never talked to anyone about it.'

Being lumped in with everyone else hurt, even though Carrie knew that the momentous shift of emotion she had experienced upon meeting him had only ever been one-sided. For him it had been a bolt of attraction that, once fulfilled, had quickly expired. Not life-changing, as it had been for her.

'I never speak about that day. I rarely talk about my father. That night at the chateau with you was the first time in a long time I've spoken to anyone about him.'

The memory of that magical night made Carrie ache all over and she hugged her arms around herself.

'All this time I've not really understood why you have so much anger towards him. But the fact that you were there, that you saw it—'

She broke off, pressing a hand to her mouth, incapable of saying anything more. She didn't know what she could say. Her head was buzzing, her thoughts too.

He'd been there.

At last it all made sense. Damon finally made sense. His hatred, his anger. That one moment, so destructive and yet so pivotal. All her questions answered in that hidden truth.

'It was awful. It was like a nightmare.'

He swallowed and looked off to the side, and when he drew a desperate breath it wasn't to draw the conversation to an end, as Carrie had fully expected, but to resume sharing.

'He would never have taken me with him if he'd thought there was any danger. He thought he'd smoothed over all the problems, that he could get everything back on track. It was meant to be a half-hour meeting and then he and I were going to spend the day together. He was going to take me to a ball game. But when we got there the crowds were already gathered. My father had security, and they tried to rush us in, but it was still chaos,' he recalled with a wince. 'The shouting, the protesting. The jeering. And then the firing. Just two shots. That was all. Everything went silent, like time stopped. And then it all came back into focus. I had been thrust to the floor. Everyone was screaming, bolting in different directions. I looked around for my father. He was lying on the floor, a few feet away from me. I thought he was okay… I started to crawl towards him, wondering why he wasn't getting up…and then I saw the blood.'

Damon's eyes swam, but his gaze was far off, back in that day. Carrie couldn't move, could only listen, even though she knew how it ended.

'All of his chest was red. I tried to stop it with my hands, but it was everywhere… pumping out of him. He said my name and reached out his hand for mine. He said "It's okay. I love you." I kept holding his hand. I didn't take my eyes off him. But he was gone by the time the paramedics got there. And I was still holding his hand.'

Tear-tracks scarred his cheeks and his breathing was uneven, and when he turned his head, his eyes locked Carrie under their dark spotlight.

'I felt his heart stop beating beneath my hands, Carrie. I felt it the moment his life ended.'

Tears flooded out of her eyes. How dark and frightening the world must have seemed to him in those immediate moments. How alone he must have felt, especially when his mother had abandoned him not long after.

She wanted to tell him she was sorry, but it felt so insufficient. She wanted to tell him she understood his pain, but she knew there could be no understanding the agony he'd been made to suffer. It made her feel useless, so achingly inadequate that there were no words that she could offer that would help or heal him.

All she could really offer was herself. Her empathy. Her emotion. The assurance that he was no longer alone.

But would he accept it?

Unable to bear the distance separating

them any longer, Carrie moved to the seat beside him. She tucked her arm under his, laced her fingers with his and pressed her face into his shoulder.

'I'm so sorry, Damon,' she whispered against his skin.

His body was rock-hard with tension, the tendons in his strong arms standing out. He said nothing, and the only move he made was to rub the pads of his fingers against her knuckles. After a few moments of sitting like that, he unlaced their fingers. Carrie shifted upwards, bracing for him to pull away from her, but he kept hold of her hand and trailed his fingertips in dazzling, sizzling patterns along her palm.

Hot sparks ignited in her stomach, excitement shifting through her veins at the slight and simple caress. It shouldn't have been so provocative, but Carrie struggled to keep her breath steady—a feat that became even harder when Damon raised her palm to his face, curling it around his cheek. The skin-to-skin contact sent a jolt through her. His stubble-roughened jaw felt delicious beneath her hand and she exhaled sharply.

He turned his head, and his dark eyes bored into hers. She didn't blink, didn't dare to breathe, didn't want to do anything that would interrupt the moment. But the need to feel more of him beneath her fingers eventually won out, and gently she allowed her thumb to trace small circles on his skin. His eyes drifted closed, his lips curving into a facsimile of a smile. When his eyes opened again it was as if they were on fire, so bright and burnished, and all Carrie craved was to be kissed by that unique heat, branded by his flame.

As if he was reading her mind, he leaned in to capture her mouth, slowly drawing his lips across hers. Her craving awakened fully, she launched herself onto his lap, curling her arms around his strong shoulders and pressing herself to him as hard as she could, matching the urgent feasting of his deep, drugging kisses.

Her blood hummed with the intimate contact. Their physical reunion was everything she had been yearning for day and night for weeks. The slide of his lips and the stroke of his hands soothed every ache in her body and answered every wish of her heart. It was sweet and sharp, deep and needy. It was everything.

And Carrie wanted every second of it—along with so much more. She wanted the tight embrace of his arms, the weight of his powerful body above hers. She wanted him to drag down her top and bare her breasts to his mouth. She wanted him to rip off her underwear and ride her to sweet fulfilment.

But he didn't want that. In his eyes she was tainted.

'Damon, wait.'

Somehow managing to disengage her lips from his sweet mouth, Carrie braced her hands against his shoulders to stay out of reach. She made an attempt to slide off his lap, because trying to think with his enormous erection straining against her was impossible, but he held her too fast.

'We shouldn't do this,' she muttered, shaking her head and trying not to look at him. Because she knew that one look at his face would cause her to crumble. 'It isn't what you want—not really. You'll regret it…just like you regret that night in Paris.'

'I won't regret it,' he said, and there was tenderness in his eyes as he forced her to meet his gaze. 'And I definitely don't regret our night in Paris.'

'But…'

Silencing her with a finger across her mouth, he continued, 'The only thing I will regret is if I don't have you in my bed again.'

Carrie wanted to believe him more than

she'd ever wanted to believe any words spoken to her, and even though she had convinced herself that all he felt about that night was remorse, the glint in his eyes and the feel of his hands on her waist told a different story.

As he slowly pulled her mouth down to his, Carrie didn't resist. Sinking into the hot, slow strokes of his tongue, she felt warmth suffuse her. Fear forgotten, she allowed her body to open to his, crushing her breasts against his chest, rubbing the apex of her thighs against his growing erection.

Through the thin fabric of her pyjamas his fingers burned where they touched, and she squirmed with her need to be free of the flimsy fabric. She reached for the hem of her top at the same moment he did, and together they pulled it over her head. Then Damon brought his mouth to her nipple, moving his tongue in a neat circle before suckling with such intensity that streaks of lightning shot straight to her molten centre. She could feel herself splintering as he offered the same worship to her other breast and knew his words had to be true. He had to want her. He could not caress her with such reverence if he did not feel something for her.

'Carrie, kiss me,' he commanded throatily, and she lowered her parted lips for him to drink from, loving the satisfied growl from the back of his throat when their mouths crashed together. 'It's not enough,' he growled against her mouth. 'I need to make love to you. I need to be inside you.'

'Upstairs?'

Her shook his head, his eyes burning with a fire she could feel thrumming beneath his skin.

'Here. Now.'

There would be no complaint from her.

Reaching down, she manoeuvred the fastening on his trousers so his erection sprang free and held his velvet length between her fingers, drawing her eyes up to watch how her touch commanded an instant reaction from him. His eyes were closed, face contorting with delight and resistance, and she grew even more bold, squeezing gently to see an even greater play of emotion, delighting in the power she possessed over him.

'Carrie…' He groaned. 'If you keep doing that you're going to kill me,' he said on a pained laugh.

She laughed, too, but released him as his hands firmly gripped her hips to rip away her shorts. She positioned herself above him, her pulse leaping with enthusiasm for what she knew was coming next, before slowly sliding herself down his length, his firm hands on her hips helping to guide her.

As she took him all the way inside her Damon's fingers bit into her skin to hold her still. His eyes locked on hers, the connection burrowing into her soul, and as he fitted within her so deeply, so perfectly, it was as though he was her missing piece.

When she could stand it no longer Carrie began to move her body, sliding up and down his remarkable length. Their mouths sought each other's, open and greedy, and as the friction built beneath Carrie's skin Damon began to caress her flesh where their bodies were connected, pressing the pad of his thumb to the bundle of nerves to intensify the sensations taking over her entire being.

His mouth sought her nipple again, coaxing it into a hard peak with the wetness of his tongue, and with those ministrations sending her hurtling towards a beautiful oblivion Carrie lifted and sank on his length with increased need. The joy of his thickness penetrating so deeply and sweetly inside her was all that mattered in the world. All she wanted was to savour their joining. To prolong it.

Damon braced an arm against the back of the sofa and thrust as she sank, and Carrie pressed her hands to his shoulders as his rhythm pushed her into territory that had her gasping and edging towards explosion. After a further thrust from Damon she tumbled over the edge in a shattering of emotion, to be quickly followed by Damon with only a single word emerging from his mouth.

'Carrie.'

CHAPTER TEN

DAMON STIRRED AND reached out an arm, only to discover that the bed was empty. His eyes flew open, his body tensing at the possibility that it had all only been another of his vivid dreams. But then he caught that light flowery scent on the sheets and knew it had been real. He and Carrie had spent the last twelve hours in bed together and, far from experiencing any guilt about that, all he felt was disappointment that he was alone amongst the tangled sheets.

Setting out in search of her, he headed straight for the kitchen, guided not just by his instincts but the scents drifting throughout the house. And sure enough there she was, her hands a blur as she diced and rolled and stirred.

Damon watched her quietly for a moment, shamelessly appreciating the sight of her in his shirt, her bare legs on display and the material made almost translucent by the slant of the late-day sun. Once again he tested his feelings, waiting to feel that sharp stab of guilt that he had broken his vow and bedded the enemy—but there was nothing of the kind.

In sharing the whole truth about the day his father had died he'd only wanted to enlighten her as to why his emotions got the better of him whenever her father was mentioned. But as he had confided in her Damon had realised he was giving her the ability to better understand him, and the freedom that had come with that, and the release he'd felt after finally sharing his harrowing experience, had been so profound that he'd wanted more of it. Had wanted to shine a light on the shadows that haunted him. To rip at the ties that bound him, the bonds of his own creation.

And kissing her had done exactly that. Kissing her had felt like freedom and peace. And it had felt so good to stop fighting his feelings and embrace them that he hadn't stopped kissing her. Hadn't stopped at all. And the surrender had been divine.

Coming up behind her, Damon slid his warm hands around her waist, liking the way she instantly melted against him. Brushing her hair aside, he grazed his lips against the tender skin of her neck, where she liked to be nuzzled, increasing the pressure as she murmured her pleasure. At the same time his fingers loosened a single button at the front of the shirt, so his hand could slide inside, teasing across her ribcage and up to her breasts. He cupped the generous swells, repeating the slide of his fingers across her nipples as her body arched in response to the sensation.

'That's the second time I've woken in a bed that you should have been in and weren't,' he whispered into her ear.

'You were sleeping and I didn't want to disturb you. I also thought you'd be glad of something to eat when you woke up,' she murmured.

'Hmm, I'm definitely hungry.' He continued the assault of his lips against her neck, shifting towards the lobe of her ear and the hollow beneath her jaw whilst his fingers played with her nipples until they were taut and she was squirming. 'You sure that's the only reason you didn't stay in bed?'

The minuscule hesitation in both her speech and her hands affirmed that his suspicion was correct. She was baking because she was anxious about something.

'I thought you might feel differently once you woke up,' she admitted, and he felt the sudden drum of tension beneath her skin. 'That you might regret…'

Damon held on to her tighter. 'I told you already… I don't regret anything.'

'If you did, I'd understand,' she continued, as though he hadn't spoken. 'You were upset, and in need of comfort, and…'

'Carrie.' He turned her, tilting her head back so their eyes connected. 'I don't regret a single thing that's happened between us.' It felt very important that she knew that. 'At one point I wanted to. Desperately. But I never did. And I don't regret today. I don't want to undo anything. I want to do it again and again and again.'

He punctuated each word with a kiss, revelling in every murmur she made before pulling her even tighter against him until there was not a single part of their bodies not touching.

'But nothing's changed,' Carrie breathed, fearful shadows dancing in her eyes. 'The past…'

'I'm not interested in the past right now.'

All that ugliness felt a long way away, and all he cared about, for the first time in a long time, was what was right in front of him. The happiness that he could reach out and take. That he *wanted* to reach out and take. Everything else was irrelevant.

'I'm only interested in this. In us.'

And in a demonstration of exactly that he lowered his mouth, the searing hot slide of his lips demanding the capitulation of hers, and slowly Carrie's body relaxed, surrendering to the compelling pressure of his mouth, the hot and hungry sweeps of his tongue. And as she rose to her tiptoes to kiss him back with an equal fervour, feeding the hunger pounding through his blood, Damon caught her around the waist, lifted her off the floor in a single swoop and set her on the marble top of the island, trapping himself between her legs and holding her tight against him.

With impatient yet deft fingers he worked apart the rest of the buttons on the shirt and then pushed the sides open, so all of her was bared to him. He palmed her breasts as he continued his assault on her lips, before dragging his mouth down her neck into a fiery exploration of her chest. Curling his tongue around her nipple, Damon sucked until she cried out, and he would have kept up the pressure—except Carrie was reaching for him, placing her hands on either side of his face and pulling his mouth back up to hers, coaxing his tongue back inside her mouth.

As they kissed with a fiery rhythm, and Carrie's desire manifested itself in moans into his mouth, Damon's own fever began to throb more insistently, even though he would have thought it impossible for him to want her more than he already did, to want her all over again when he'd spent hours already tasting and touching her in bed.

But knowing how and where she liked to be caressed, and how it felt to slide inside her, was an electrifying familiarity. It was as thrilling to him to know the explosive orgasm that awaited him as it had been to touch her for the first time.

Too aroused, too crazed, to play any longer, he pulled her to the very edge of the counter and fastened his hands to her hips, feeling her wetness as he positioned himself at her entrance. To know that she was that eager, that ready for him, made him even harder, and as he drove powerfully into her Carrie arched, her hands clasping his shoulders, her nails biting into his skin and her green eyes exploding with dazzling emerald colour.

With each strong and claiming thrust she clung tighter to him, her moans ripped from deep within her throat, the sounds unleashing such a fire within him that Damon didn't know if he would ever get enough of her to put it out. But then he plunged into her a final time and they crashed into their climax together, and the storm that broke inside him was so intense that every inch of him pulsed with a fulfilment unlike anything else he'd ever known.

Carrie's heart pounded in a reckless, uneven rhythm, but it was matched by the frenzied beats pulsing in Damon's chest. Burying her face in the sweet-smelling nook of his neck, she inhaled the scent of his skin and splayed her fingers against the smooth, strong muscles of his back as she waited for the violent lashes of the orgasm he had given her to subside into pleasing, teasing ripples of silky sensation.

Damon had turned her inside out half a dozen times already, but none of those moments had been as passionately explosive at that one.

And she knew why.

'I'm not interested in the past. Only this. Us.'

They were the magic words she'd been longing to hear since… Oh, only since the first moment they'd met. And they had unlocked so much within her—everything she'd been trying to contain. Hope. Need. Desire.

Lying awake in his arms a short while earlier, Carrie had been thrumming with nervousness, convinced that, regardless of what he had said about not regretting anything, once he woke he would feel remorse for making love to her again. She had fled his bed solely to spare herself the hideousness of that moment. But then he'd come after her and issued those words, and with the promise of them glowing in his eyes, the truth of them burning in his hungry kiss, the uncertainty she felt had quietened, slipping almost entirely from her mind, leaving her free to give in to her need for him, her feelings for him.

She knew it was a risk, because she couldn't give her body without engaging her heart. But if there was a chance that they could be *something* to one another, a chance to explore all that moved and burned between them, a chance that she could better know the complicated, emotional, compassionate, sexy man that was Damon Meyer, that was a chance Carrie wanted to take. For herself and for their child.

She wouldn't waste time fearing it or questioning it. She would simply accept it. Embrace it.

In spite of the chaos happening in the outside world, Carrie and Damon enjoyed a blissful few days in the seclusion of his Ojai estate.

Damon showed her all around the house and the gorgeous land surrounding it, walking her through orange and avocado groves and sunflower gardens. She felt such peace and contentment that in certain moments she even managed to forget about the media craze that had propelled them there in the first place, but generally it was never far from her mind, and when she emerged from the bathroom one morning, her body still humming from their steamy session in the shower, and saw Damon's frowning expression as he hung up the phone, her stomach clenched.

'What's happened?'

'Nothing bad.' Strolling towards her, he pressed a reassuring kiss to her forehead. 'It was my aunt Bree, reminding me about my cousin's birthday dinner tonight.' He sighed. 'I suppose since I'm here I should make the effort to go.'

'You don't normally make the effort?' Carrie asked, slightly surprised, as she'd seen the fondness with which he talked of his cousins. The most breathtaking smile had lit his face when he'd shared stories of growing up with them in Ojai, although it hadn't escaped her notice that most of those tales hailed from the time when his father had been alive, further proving just how much his world had changed, darkened, in the days after he'd died.

'I'm not in Ojai that often.'

'LA isn't that far away.'

'I'm not always in LA either,' he countered, turning away from her with a look that expressed aggravation at being questioned and striding to the closet, snatching the first tee shirt he touched.

'And that's what's stopped you from showing up? Geography?'

Carrie's eyes narrowed as he kept his back to her, his muscles tellingly taut, and her senses clanged with the warning that they had stumbled into difficult emotional terrain. And even though it was obvious that Damon wanted to retreat and hide from whatever feelings had been stirred up, Carrie wanted to know and understand them. To help him.

Closing the space between them, she ran her hand down his tense arm. 'Damon? Talk to me.'

It was a long moment before he spoke. 'I've got very good at keeping myself separate, okay?' he admitted roughly. 'After what happened, I didn't want to be close to anyone. I didn't want to take that risk.'

He was scared to love in case he lost again,

Carrie realised with a painful twist of her heart.

'That's understandable. You went through something awful, losing your father and then having your mother walk away too. You're trying to keep yourself safe.' She paused, wondering how far her new privileges extended…if she could push a little deeper without scaring him into shutting her out too. 'The only problem is that doing that stops you experiencing good stuff too.'

Carrie knew that from personal experience. Fear had made her hide herself away and she'd missed out on so much… If she hadn't taken that chance with Damon in Paris she'd have missed out on something extraordinary. And if Damon couldn't conquer his fear, what did that mean for the future? Would he hold back from his child to avoid being hurt? And what about *them*?

He'd made no promises, and Carrie hadn't asked for any. They were simply acting on their mutual attraction and enjoying it. But if he remained a hostage to his fear of loving and losing she knew there was not even the hope of it turning into something more.

'I've kept my distance for so long, Carrie…' He sighed. 'I wouldn't know how to change even if I wanted to.'

She smiled, his words giving her hope that he *wanted* to change. 'I think you start by showing up at that party and let it go from there.'

He fired her a look of scepticism. 'Just show up? After years of not showing up?'

'Yes. And they'll be happy. The people who truly love you just want you with them, and everything that's gone before will become irrelevant once they have you back.' She slid against him, worked herself into his arms. 'They'll understand—even if you can never find the words to explain it to them.'

'Not everyone is like you, Carrie. Not everyone is compassionate and willing to forgive.'

'If your aunt didn't want you there she wouldn't have called. That was her telling you that she loves you and is there for you. Family is important, Damon. You have people who love you. Don't shut them out. And if not for yourself, do it for our child. Because he or she deserves to have family and love in its life.'

He looked away, but she knew he was thinking. Considering.

'Would you come with me?' he asked.

Carrie hesitated. Having trained himself to rely on only himself, Damon asking for her support was monumental, but as much as Carrie wanted to help him reconnect with his family, she was wary.

'Is that such a good idea? Me with your father's family?'

Nerves rattled beneath her skin at the thought. She didn't think anything could be as bad as Damon's reaction to her identity, but walking into a room where every single person had lost a cherished family member because of actions kick-started by her father would be unpleasant.

She would be *Sterling Randolph's daughter* once again.

'You'd have nothing to fear from anyone in that house tonight,' he promised.

The weight in her stomach lessened only slightly, but she smiled anyway. 'Of course I'll go with you.'

The truth was, she realised in that moment, she would go anywhere with him that he asked her to. Any time he asked. Even if it meant facing her own fears and experiencing discomfort.

Because supporting him was more important.

It was a depth of feeling that scared her, because whenever she had allowed herself to feel with such ardency in the past, her heart and her spirit had been crushed. And, with the way her feelings for Damon grew so rapidly each day, any damage to her heart by him could prove irreparable.

Damon had been right when he'd said she had nothing to fear from his family.

Everyone was warm and welcoming from the moment she walked through the door. If they were surprised that she, of all the women in the world, was accompanying Damon, they didn't show it.

She was ushered inside, the strawberry shortcake she had made especially for the dinner was gushed over and added to the waiting table of culinary treats, and her bakery business was queried with immense interest. Immediately put at ease, she transferred her attention to Damon, watching his interactions.

He was tentative at first, falling into what she imagined was his usual pattern of holding himself back and keeping everyone at a distance, but eventually he grew easier, laughing fondly with his cousin Noah and reliving long-ago boyhood exploits. And in watching his family, Carrie saw her words had been right. They were delighted to have him there and to have more of him than he'd previously been willing to share.

Happiness warmed her insides. Knowing how tough it must be to face that fear of loving and losing, she couldn't be more in awe of him for attempting to break the habits engraved in him over a lifetime.

After dinner, when the family had dispersed to different areas of the house, Carrie found herself admiring the display of family photographs on a sideboard in the large hall. In a gold frame was a picture of Damon and Noah, young and tanned, heads pressed together, smiling at the camera with such joy and the lightness that Carrie now knew Damon had lost when he'd lost his father. Then her gaze snagged on a different photo at the back of the display—a photo boasting a face that was easily recognisable: Jacob Meyer.

As she took in the lively eyes, bright smile and broad shoulders, the lump growing in her throat felt as if it was wrapped in barbed wire. Standing in front of him, with his father's arms loosely draped around him, was a young Damon.

'Damon's quite like him, don't you think?'

Carrie jolted. She hadn't heard his Aunt Bree approach, and to be caught red-handed, holding the picture of Jacob... 'I'm sorry. I didn't mean to...'

'It's fine.' Bree offered her a reassuring smile. 'You're only looking at the photographs. It's why I have them out.' She picked up the frame Carrie had set down in a panic, looked at it lovingly.

'You must miss him terribly.'

'I do. He was a good brother.'

'I'm sorry for what happened to him...for the part my father played.'

'Thank you.' Bree touched a hand to her arm. 'Although you have nothing to apologise for—you were a little girl. And your father—whatever part he played—didn't pull the trigger. It was a tragedy, and no one suffered for it more than him.' She stared intently at the snapshot of Damon. 'It's wonderful to see him finding some happiness at last—to see him letting himself be happy'

'I want him to be happy,' Carrie heard herself say, unsure why the subject of his happiness brought such sadness crashing down on her.

He had opened up to her and let her in, but there was still so much she didn't know, and the future seemed so unclear. Was Damon really ready to let go of the past and the animosity he carried because of it? Would he be able to regain the spirt of that laughing, carefree boy in the photograph? Would he ever fully open his heart?

And was Carrie risking her own heart by opening it to him?

CHAPTER ELEVEN

'THERE HASN'T BEEN anything new about us online today,' Carrie mentioned, taking a bite from her meal as they ate dinner on the veranda, the sun setting behind them.

Bathed in the dying rays of light, her black hair shone and her eyes danced with colour, and Damon ached for the moment when he would lead her inside, tease her from her clothes and tumble her onto the bed.

'I noticed. I told you they would move on.'

'I guess that means we'll be going home soon, then?'

Damon faltered at the question. He hadn't given any thought to returning home. He'd been too busy enjoying Carrie and the intimate routine they'd established in their hideaway to give any consideration to leaving. And as her question rolled around his mind the thought of returning to reality was an uneasy one.

'We could… Although I have another idea.' He thought quickly, the plan taking shape in his mind with such ease that he couldn't halt his smile. 'Come to Paris with me.'

'Paris?'

'Yes. I have a few meetings arranged, but I don't need to work the whole time, and there's Jean-Pierre's daughter's wedding at the chateau. It could be fun to go back there together,' he coaxed.

Carrie watched him, a smile tugging at the corners of her mouth. 'You really want me to go with you?'

'Yes, I do,' he replied, realising as he gave the assurance just how badly he did want her company.

A happy blush rose in her cheeks. 'I'll call Marina and my grandmother, and if they're happy to cover for me at the bakery for a little while longer, then, yes, I'll come to Paris with you.'

Three days later they were back in the City of Light, and Damon felt an unexpected pleasure in returning to the city where his connection with Carrie had been forged and their child had been conceived.

With the combination of jet lag and her pregnancy fatigue Carrie was exhausted when they arrived, so Damon insisted that she remain at the penthouse and rest whilst he attended his meetings. She laughed at his overprotectiveness, then agreed, and he parted from her reluctantly with a long kiss. But his concern for her meant that more than once during his meetings his mind strayed to her.

He returned to the penthouse to check on her mid-afternoon, when he had a short break in business, and was relieved to see the colour had returned to her cheeks and the dark crescents beneath her eyes were fading. By the following morning Carrie was back to her bright, energetic self, and after an early breakfast meeting Damon happily devoted the rest of the day to her.

Life was different with Carrie at his side. It was fuller, brighter. It had never occurred to him that he was missing out on something extraordinary by not sharing his time and his space with someone, but she filled gaps in his life and within himself that he hadn't known existed. With her, he saw a different way to be, a different way to live. He'd reconnected with his family because of her. He had faced those awful traumatic memories and felt their power over him lessen. She was light and air, breaking up the darkness that had surrounded him, and with her he focused on the good, dwelling less and less on the past and feeling less burdened because of it.

His feelings for Carrie had deepened and grown so substantially that increasingly Damon caught himself contemplating the future, looking ahead to when they would be joined by their little one with excitement running through his veins and a smile on his face.

But even as that sense of pleasure grew, a corresponding unease stacked in his stomach. The Caldwell deal winner would be announced any day, and Damon's certainty that vengeance was the right—the *only*—thing had slackened. He'd been unable to forget what he'd learned about Sterling Randolph. Those facts surfaced in his mind randomly, but always with the same prodding at his conscience, and then he'd look at Carrie and the stab would pierce even deeper.

He'd always looked towards the day of the Caldwell announcement as a day of triumph for him and a day of reckoning for Sterling, but Damon was starting to wonder if it would be his own day of reckoning instead...

As Carrie emerged from the bedroom Damon turned from his contemplation of the city below them and the look that filled his eyes threatened to unbalance her. No one had ever surveyed her with such unrestrained appreciation and appetite, and even though her first thought when she'd appraised herself in the mirror that morning had been that she looked beautiful, Carrie had attributed that to the hair and make-up experts who'd readied her for this exclusive wedding so she didn't tire herself. But the way Damon was looking at her made her feel as though it was far more than that. That in some way she was essential to him.

'You're ravishing.'

He smiled with a wolfish curl of his lips, leaving her in no doubt that he was envisaging all the ways he would like to ravish her. Carrie made a mental note not to let him touch her before they were out through the door, because given how turned on she felt under his heated attention, and how sensational he looked in his tuxedo, it was unlikely she would be able to resist. It was also entirely possible she would be the one to drag him to the floor and set about tasting every inch of his body.

'And you're mine.'

'All yours,' she breathed, melting beneath his words and feeling in that moment how very much she did belong to him, how she ached for him to be unequivocally, officially hers.

When he surveyed her with so much delicacy and awe, and uttered sentiments like that, it made her believe that was what he wanted too. But the truth was she just didn't know.

The future Damon saw for them, if any, was a mystery, and Carrie was too scared to ask. Her mind was alive with hopeful fantasies of the life they could share together—beautiful and blissful visions of family and love and laughter—but the memory of past disappointments was never far away. And although Damon had opened himself up to her, and given her reasons to believe in him, she found it a struggle to trust entirely. Especially when sometimes it felt as if he was still holding things back.

He'd unburdened himself about his father, but in certain moments he still seemed to carry leaden thoughts that cast his whole expression in anguish. When she asked him he'd tell her it was nothing, but Carrie was certain she could detect turmoil in him, and she was afraid it was about them…that even with the best of intentions the thought of a future with her—a Randolph—was too much to overcome.

Worries like that should, she knew, give her pause for thought, but it was hard not to want everything with Damon when their child's heart beat in her body, and when every time she thought of their child, or looked into Damon's burnished gaze, she was aware of how much of a capacity for love she had.

And those desires of her heart only grew larger in her mind later, as she watched the wedding at Chateau Margaux. As she watched the bride and groom clasp each other's hands, stare lovingly into each other's eyes and pledge their eternal and unfailing love to each other. With tears shining in her own eyes, Carrie knew she wanted exactly that. She'd always yearned for that kind of love, and ever since Damon had come into her life she'd longed for it with him.

It was all she could dwell on as they moved from the ceremony into the celebrations.

'You're quiet tonight,' Damon commented as he led her onto the dance floor, pulling her in close to the heat of his body. 'Are you feeling unwell?'

'I'm fine,' she assured him. 'I'm just enjoying the wedding. I never thought I'd be here again.'

'I've never wanted somebody as badly as I wanted you that night. I'd never wanted *anything* as much as I wanted you. And from that moment to this one that's never changed.'

His actions constantly told her that, but to

hear it from his lips was an altogether different kind of delight, and Carrie felt herself blush.

'When we get back to California, I want you to look at properties with me,' he told her.

'Okay. I'd love to.'

'Good. Because I was thinking that you might have some interest in living there too.'

Stunned, she stopped moving and could only stare up at him. 'You're… Are you asking me to live with you?'

'Well, we are having a baby together,' he said with a deep smile. 'And I know what I said before…but it's different now.' He dropped his mouth so it brushed her ear and said, very intently, 'I don't want to miss a second of any of this, Carrie. And I don't want to be apart from you if I don't need to be.'

His admission gave her the freedom to speak some of her truth. 'I don't want to be without you either.'

'So that's a yes?'

It was everything she could want. Her heart felt close to bursting.

'Yes!' She beamed.

When Carrie woke the next morning she was curled up in Damon's arms. His fingers were absentmindedly stroking down her hair, and beneath her ear she could feel and hear the steady beats of his heart.

Memories of the previous night filtered through her mind: the way he'd held her as they watched the fireworks display at the chateau, how he'd carried her up to the penthouse from the car, the slow and sensual way he'd undressed her, kissing every single inch of her, and how her feelings of safety and happiness had deepened, settling across her like a blanket.

'I know you're awake. Your breathing's changed.'

She smiled, pressing a kiss to the warm skin of his chest. 'Good morning. Is it late?'

'It's a little after ten. What do you say to breakfast on the terrace and then a leisurely Sunday wandering around the Marais? You said you wanted to explore it a bit more.'

Resting her chin on his chest, she gazed up at him. 'That sounds perfect.'

She bestowed a kiss upon his lips, and then another. And as the taste of him was so good she couldn't stop herself from stealing another. But they could never stop with a single touch. Within seconds their limbs were tangled, their bodies curved into the shape of each other.

Carrie trailed kisses over his torso, scratching her teeth against his nipple and drawing from him that groan she loved so much. Her hands explored his taut, hot skin, seeking his hard length, and as she found it she stroked over him, feeling brave and bold and sure, and smiling as he bit out a ragged curse. Damon punished her laughter with a hard kiss, rolling her onto her back and moving her hands above her head, pinning them with his own. Teasing her body with his, he made her wait until she was squirming before sinking his length into her.

They made it to the Marais a short while later. One of the oldest districts in France, its narrow cobblestoned streets, hidden courtyards and tranquil gardens offered a glimpse of what Paris had been centuries ago, and Carrie was immediately enthralled by its beauty. They explored the maze-like streets and Damon was in his element, admiring the stunning architecture of the ancient aristocratic mansions. He showed Carrie the intricacies of the designs and she relished his enjoyment, his passion.

Hand in hand, they strolled through the Place des Vosges, the sunshine on their faces, before investigating the boutiques and galleries lining the square. With help from Damon, Carrie selected gifts for her grandmother and

Marina, to thank them for taking over for her at the bakery whilst she'd been away, and Damon sought her opinion on works of art that he liked as he considered adding to what she learned was an extensive collection.

When their legs were begging for relief they stopped for an early dinner at a restaurant on the banks of the Seine and, closeted at a secluded corner table, they watched as the fading light sent its last sparkles across the slow-moving river and the city became illuminated as darkness descended.

It had been the most wonderful day, Carrie reflected later, when they were back at the penthouse. For the first time in weeks the future seemed clear. Like seeing far-off mountains on a cloudless day, she could see the life that lay ahead of her: making a home with Damon, welcoming their child in less than six months, becoming the type of family she had always wanted for her child. And for herself.

So what if he hadn't actually told her that he loved her? After everything he'd been through Carrie knew it wouldn't be easy for Damon to say those words. But all his actions showed how much he cared for her, and actions spoke louder than words, didn't they?

But if she truly believed that, why could

she feel small frissons of apprehension skittering through her mind…?

Damon couldn't sleep, and the glowing numbers on the clock showed him just how long his tormented thoughts had kept him awake. Unable to stand it any longer, he extricated himself from Carrie's arms and slid from the warm bed, pulling on his clothes and heading for the building's luxury pool.

One hour and well over a hundred lengths later, Damon's muscles pleaded for a respite, but he continued to cut through the water, pushing himself harder, determined to excise the anguish from his mind.

The path before him had once been so straight and simple. Everything had been about organising Sterling Randolph's undoing. But now there was Carrie and their baby, and life with her was so good and easy. Every time she'd looked at him that day it had been with stars in her eyes and a smile brighter than the sunshine, and that had caused his heart to twist. Because he wanted to bask in the love she so readily offered, to take her hand and run into the future with her. But how could he when seizing that future with her would demand he abandon his revenge, let go of everything that had driven and anchored him for all his adult life?

Damon had imagined himself doing it—picking up the phone to make the call or send the email that would end it all—but, as much as a piece of him yearned to do exactly that, he knew he wouldn't. *Couldn't.* Because if he didn't finish this Randolph would get away with it. Again. He would never be made to pay for his sins. And Damon couldn't stomach that injustice. He deserved that victory—for himself and his father.

Carrie meant so much to him, but she wasn't more important than his revenge.

And it wasn't as though love came with any guarantees. Throwing away all that he'd worked for to be with Carrie didn't ensure them a future together. He could lose her, just like he'd lost his mother, and he certainly didn't have much faith in his capacity to love her the way she deserved to be loved. Look at how easy he'd found it to close himself off from his family and remain that way.

Carrie believed he could be redeemed, but he would only disappoint her in the long run, and if he lost both Carrie *and* his shot at revenge he'd have nothing. It would have all been for nothing.

Finishing a length, Damon came to rest

at the side of the pool, his chest aching with exertion and the weight of his decision. He was at a crossroads. He could have Carrie and their baby and the promise of a bright future or he could have his revenge. There was no way he could have both. And if he made the wrong choice, he ran the risk of ending up with nothing at all.

The email arrived in Damon's inbox at ten the following morning.

He'd won the Caldwell contract. All he needed to do was sign it and Sterling Randolph would be ruined. Revenge would finally be his...

But suddenly Damon knew how wrong that was.

There was no victory in vengeance. There was only more pain and loss. And he wasn't prepared to lose Carrie just to settle a decades-old score. Because having her in his life was more important than anything else. *She* was all that he needed to be happy.

How he had ever doubted that he could love her was beyond him, because in that second he knew with blinding clarity that he could and he did. And to think of how close he'd come to destroying that—and to wreaking havoc on her father's life—was so horrifying he was almost choking on it!

But fortunately it wasn't too late for them. She had no idea of the monumental mistake he'd been so close to making, so he still had the chance to claim the future with her that he so desperately wanted.

And he wanted to start straight away by telling her how much he loved her and how grateful he was for her.

He was getting to his feet when his phone rang. Isobel's name was flashing on the screen.

Knowing with absolute certainty the way forward, Damon answered immediately, speaking before she did.

'Put a hold on that contract,' he directed her.

'A—a hold…?' Isobel stammered disbelievingly. 'But you only just—'

'I'll explain later. Just put the hold on it,' he repeated urgently, hanging up.

He located Carrie, sitting out on the terrace with the sun streaming over her, looking so beautiful his heart skipped a beat. She was staring at the phone in her hand. As he approached, his feelings ready to burst out of him, she lifted her head—and what he saw had his ecstatic heart slowing. Her face had lost all its colour and her eyes were clouded with a suspicion and anger that only sharpened as she looked at him.

With a sick feeling drilling down from his chest to his stomach Damon knew that he *was* too late. Somehow she knew everything.

He'd finally realised he loved her. Only now he was going to lose her. And there was no one to blame but himself.

Carrie stared up at Damon, the information that had just been communicated to her by her brother Xander spinning in her mind.

It wasn't possible, she thought frantically. It *couldn't* be possible.

But the dots were joining up to form a horrifying picture in her mind, and in her chest her heart was thundering with a dread that was quickly boring into every bone in her body.

'Carrie…' Damon started, his expression constricting.

'My brother just called me,' she said, managing to speak through the leaden weight on her chest. 'My father's in hospital. They think he's had a heart attack. Because you won the Caldwell contract and he didn't.'

She didn't take her eyes off him, wanting

to see every flicker and flutter of emotion. Wanting to see the truth.

'Did you know that he was in the running for the project too?' she asked.

Damon hesitated only slightly before nodding once.

'And did you also know that there's been tension over his leadership at the Randolph Corporation? That he needed to win that contract to stay in control there?'

The silence between them stretched tight as she waited for him to answer. The weight on her chest tripled as she beseeched him to say something, *anything*, that would make more sense than the notions running through her mind. But hot, angry tears were already brewing in her eyes, because she could feel, like the tremors of an earthquake, that the truth was about to be revealed, and that it would bring the beautiful life she had been living crashing down.

Damon had been lying to her. Manipulating her. He was as bad as all the other men she'd ever known. And on some level she wasn't even surprised. She'd known all along that he was withholding something from her. Known she'd given over her trust too easily and freely…that she had pinned her hopes on a man destined to disappoint her. She should have listened to those repeated warnings from her head.

'That's why you wanted that contract,' she said, realising the extent of his deception. 'To get back at him. To ruin him.'

Carrie had expected it to strike her with the force of a wrecking ball, but it didn't. It was much slower, sinking into her like a thousand thorns, a pain that pushed in deeper and deeper until it was all she could feel.

'The board are going to vote him out. He's going to lose everything because of this, Damon. Because of *you*. How could you do this?'

She stared at him, but before he even came close to mustering up an answer, another thought barrelled into her.

'Am *I* part of this revenge?' she demanded, aghast at the thought that she'd somehow allowed herself to be used against her father. That she'd been a pawn in his twisted vendetta. 'Is that why you changed your mind about wanting to be involved with the baby? So you could take his family too?'

Damon opened his mouth, but she was already shaking her head, warding off anything he might say.

'On second thoughts, don't bother answering. It's not like I can trust anything you say or do, is it?'

Carrie paced away from him, sucking in lungful after lungful of air, but it wasn't enough. Every inch of her chest burned…every beat of her heart ached.

'At no point did you think about how doing this would affect me or our child…'

'I have thought about that—' he began.

But Carrie didn't want to hear his defence. It would only be more lies!

'No, you have not! Because if you had you would have stopped. You would have called off whatever you were doing before it got to this point. But all you've thought about is yourself. What *you* feel. What *you* need. If you loved me the way I love you—if you had any feelings for me at all—you wouldn't have done this.'

But he obviously didn't love her. Because, just like her father, he had placed his business and his thirst for revenge ahead of her and their child. Ahead of the life they could have shared. And that was shattering.

'You are a selfish man, Damon. You never deserved a single piece of my heart.'

And it was with that agonising realisation that the anger drained out of her and all she felt was the pain of her heartbreak, the disappointments of the past and the present colliding, and it was so excruciating it threatened to cleave her in two.

She knew she could no longer stay there. Without looking at Damon, she ran for the door.

'Carrie, don't leave...please.'

His anguished plea followed her, clawing at her already shredded heart.

'You don't understand everything. Let me explain... Where are you going to go?'

She threw open the door without looking back at him. 'Far away from you.'

CHAPTER TWELVE

DAMON STARED AT the gravestone bearing his beloved father's name. He was holding the Caldwell contract in his hands. But it was still unsigned and it would remain that way—because whatever triumph he'd thought he could achieve it would never have been more than a hollow victory.

He'd brought Sterling Randolph to his knees. He was attached to wires in a hospital bed, being forced to reckon with his mortality and the fallibility of his power, but it hadn't healed anything within him.

His father was gone, and nothing could change that. There was nothing in the universe capable of making that absence bearable. It was a loss that had to be borne, a grief that needed to be endured. That cavernous hole inside of him still existed and anger continued to roil in his gut.

He had realised it in time and yet also too late.

Because he'd not completely stained his soul, but he had lost Carrie. He had destroyed everything good between them, decimated all the faith she'd pushed past her fears to place in him.

Carrie, who had eased the burden of his emotions, who'd made every day bright and beautiful. Who'd shown him that the past was far less important than the present and the future. But when he'd had the chance to prove that to her he had failed.

He wished he'd realised the error of his ways earlier, halted his plans sooner!

He didn't blame her for storming off, refusing to hear him out. He had let her down in the worst way.

Something splintered inside him as he finally faced up to what a gigantic fool he'd been. He had clung to his anger when he should have been grabbing Carrie with both hands and holding on tight. Because having the person you loved in your life and by your side was the greatest gift imaginable. By refusing to let go of the past, he'd given away his future. *Their* future.

'Damon?'

He hadn't heard the car behind him pull up, and he didn't recognise its owner through the pouring rain until she hurried to his side and lifted her wide umbrella over him.

'Why are you standing here in this rain? You're soaked through,' cried his Aunt Bree, casting a horrified eye over his drenched clothes before examining his face. 'What's the matter?'

'He's gone,' he said, unable to move his eyes from the grave. 'I lost him and now I've lost her too.'

'Her? Who…? Carrie? Are you talking about Carrie? What happened?'

Through aching, gritty eyes—because he had not rested since Carrie had stormed out of the apartment in Paris—he looked at his aunt and saw that same willingness to listen and support that had always been there. Only he had been too scared to accept it. Too scared to let her close in case he lost her too. But loss was a part of love, and Carrie was right. By closing himself off emotionally, he'd closed himself from so many other good things.

Taking a deep breath, he began to talk, telling her everything until there were no more words left.

'I was a stupid, foolish man, Aunt Bree.'

She sighed. 'You may not be able to change anything about your father being gone, but you can change things with Carrie. She's not lost to you, Damon, not if you don't want her to be.'

And suddenly he remembered Carrie's words. She'd said that people who loved someone— truly loved someone—would never stop waiting for them to come back. In that moment his aunt had proved how wise and right Carrie had been, and Damon found himself hoping they remained true of Carrie. Because without a doubt he knew that without her that hole in him would never go away.

She was the only one capable of making him whole and there was no one on the planet— *no one*—who could love her better or harder than he did.

But before he could go to her as a man deserving of her love and beg for her forgiveness, there was somebody else he had to face first.

Damon got to his feet as the door opened and Sterling Randolph was shown into the lounge. His heart thudded beneath his suit jacket. This was the showdown he had always anticipated, yet it would play out nothing like the way he'd once imagined.

Randolph reached the table and cast his eyes around—dark green, just like Carrie's— taking in the silence, the emptiness. When his gaze settled back on Damon, he arched a brushy eyebrow.

'You didn't want an audience for your moment of triumph?'

'There's no need for an audience,' Damon informed him levelly, retaking his seat. 'We're just having a conversation.'

'Really? How civilised. Ending it all with a conversation.' Sterling took a sip of the drink the waiter had deposited on the table. 'So, this is the part where you explain that you have me right where you want me?'

'No,' Damon said after a beat, looking him straight in the eye. 'This is the part where I tell you that I'm done.'

'Excuse me?'

'I'm done,' Damon repeated, feeling the last of that leaden weight lift off his shoulders as he breathed the words into reality. 'Done with hunting you, competing with you, undermining your business. Done.'

Carrie put down the phone, her body ringing with disbelief. Her father had actually taken the time and effort to call her to reassure her about his health and, whilst that was astonishing in itself, it was the information he'd shared about Damon that had left her reeling.

He had withdrawn his bid for the Caldwell building!

He'd refused to say anything more, even when Carrie had pushed him for details, adding only that Damon was a good man and she should speak with him herself.

Which was easier said than done.

Because she hadn't spoken or communicated with Damon at all since storming out of his Paris penthouse.

Her hand moved to caress her bump, as it did every time her thoughts rewound to that awful day. To those awful, heartbreaking revelations and her own unforgiving reaction.

And didn't this just prove what she was already struggling with? That she had been too quick to judge Damon? That she had listened to her own hurt and anger and fear instead of listening to him, the man she had fallen in love with? He'd been in despair— she'd seen it with her own eyes—and yet still she'd walked away. At their first real test as a couple she had failed him. She'd accused Damon of destroying them, but Carrie could no longer hide from the truth that she had too.

She knew she had her reasons for reacting as she had—she was still suffering from the way things had been with her father and Nate and her fear of going through anything similar again—but Damon had already proved he wasn't like them. She should have trusted in that…in him.

And she needed to tell him that. Now. Before another day ended. She needed him to know how sorry she was for walking out on him when he'd so obviously needed her, and that she wanted to be there for him now. Because, whilst she had no idea what was going on, for him to have turned down the Caldwell contract she knew something was happening—something big!

She picked up the phone to call him before deciding against it. A phone call wasn't enough. She needed to see him, to touch him, to look into his beautiful burnished eyes as she said the words.

Snatching up her car keys, she hurried to her front door, trying to work out how long the drive to LA would take so late in the afternoon, but as she pulled the door open she froze—because there he was, his hand raised and poised to knock.

'Damon…' she breathed, stunned by the beautiful sight of him.

'You're on your way out?'

'Only to find you,' she said, her eyes drinking him in, feeling in her bones how much she had missed him. 'To apologise.'

He shook his head. 'You have nothing to be sorry about Carrie. I'm the one who needs to apologise. Can I come in?' he asked tentatively.

'Of course.' She moved back to let him enter and he followed her into the living space. 'How are you? Both of you?' His eyes had dropped to the bump beneath her loose tee.

'We're good. Healthy.' She smoothed her hands over her stomach. 'I'm starting to show now.'

'I see that. It's beautiful.'

As he raised his gaze to her face Carrie immediately fell headlong into the golden beam of his eyes…eyes that were no longer shadowed, but clear and serene. Her heart started to pound, trying to punch itself free from her chest and into his hands.

'You're beautiful,' he added.

With those words, her emotions started to unravel, and tears built behind her eyes.

Damon stepped closer, taking her hands in his and holding them against his chest. 'I'm so sorry, Carrie. There are so many things that I want to say to you, but that's the most important. That you know how deeply I regret everything. I've made some big mistakes and

I've hurt you badly and that was never what I wanted to do.'

Exhaling a shaky breath, he continued. 'You're everything to me, Carrie. When I think about the future, I think only about you and the life we could have together. A house here, overlooking the ocean, weekends in Ojai, our baby being born and growing up… I want that future with you. I want a beautiful life with you. I want to try every day to be a man deserving of your love, a man that you and our child can believe in and rely on, no matter what.'

Carrie couldn't stay quiet a second longer—not when the harsh words she'd levelled at him on that horrible day echoed between them.

'Damon, I should never have said that you weren't deserving of my heart,' she said, shame burning through her. She moved in closer, clutching at him. 'I was wrong to say that. I was wrong not to give you the chance to speak, to explain what you were going through, and I've regretted it ever since. But I got scared and I reacted. All I could see was that another man I loved had lied to me and put his ambition ahead of our relationship. All the fears I had about trusting you roared back to the surface. But you deserved better than that from me…because you've proved time and time again that I can trust you.'

He wiped at the tears on her cheeks. 'You had every right to be furious with me. I hurt you. I let you down. But I really hope that beautiful, understanding heart of yours has the capacity to forgive me one more time, because I am in love with you, Carrie. I have loved you since those very first moments in Paris. I was just too scared of risking my heart to truly let myself see it and feel it. But losing you in Paris woke me up, and I know now that the real risk lies in not loving you as hard as I can for as long as I can, and in not telling you how much I love you every single day.'

It was everything she'd wanted to hear, and all the sweeter for everything they'd been through.

'I love you, too, Damon. And I've missed you so much.'

With a sigh of relief he released her hands to curl his arms around her and, burying his face in her river of dark hair, he held her tightly against him. 'I'm sorry it took me so long to figure it out,' he whispered.

'No more apologies. The past is done. From now on we just look forward.'

His answering smile was breathtaking. 'I like the sound of that. And in that spirit…'

He caught her completely by surprise as he dropped to his knee, producing a small velvet box.

'I love you, Carrie. I love you more than I thought it was possible to love. And, having known the pain of waking up without you beside me, I never want to be without you again. All I want now and every day, for the rest of my life, is you and our child. To spend every day with you and to spend all those days making you as happy as its possible to be. So, Caroline Miller-Randolph, will you marry me?'

Carrie had so many loving things she wanted to say to him, so many feelings burning in her heart that she wanted him to know, but there was only one word she was actually able to say, and she knew it was the only word that mattered.

'Yes.'

Damon slid the ring onto her finger and sealed the move with a kiss, then another kiss to her stomach, and a final one to her lips.

'I love you,' he said again, and it was a promise.

Excitement exploded inside her like a constellation of fireworks. 'I don't think I'll ever get tired of hearing that.'

'Good. Because I plan on saying it a lot. And showing you a lot too,' he added, boosting her up in his arms.

Before she drifted into the paradise of his lips melting against hers, Carrie stole another look at the ring sparkling on her finger.

Maybe it hadn't always unfolded like the classic fairy-tale she'd wanted, but it had been their story—hers and Damon's—and she couldn't wait for the life of love and laughter and togetherness that would come next.

* * * * *

If you were blown away by
An Heir for the Vengeful Billionaire
then be sure to watch out for
Rosie Maxwell's next story
from Harlequin Presents!